SABOTAGE THE SHUTTLE!

"Don't move," Steve shouted. "Or you're a dead man."

Marcelo stopped. His eyes tried to see beyond the lights.

Seconds remained. Marcelo was weighing what to do next. Push the button and four heroic people would die for nothing. But he would have his revenge if nothing else.

"You win," Marcelo said softly. "With seconds to spare."

Then Marcelo moved suddenly, jumping for the instruments. Steve fired and missed. . . .

Books In the Counterforce Series
by Dan Streib

COUNTERFORCE

THE TRIDENT HIJACKING

DEATH SHUTTLE

DAN STREIB

FAWCETT GOLD MEDAL • NEW YORK

A Fawcett Gold Medal Book
Published by Ballantine Books

Library of Congress Catalog Card Number: 83-90007

ISBN 0-449-12389-8

Printed in Canada

First Ballantine Books Edition: September 1983

Chapter 1

SOLID rocket boosters strapped to the sides of the delta-shaped space shuttle ignited in twin tornadoes of power. The three main engines gulped liquid hydrogen and oxygen, enough to fill sixteen swimming pools, and erupted in giant, fierce yellow fireballs and raging storm clouds of white smoke.

The combination rocket-spacecraft-airplane roared upward and away from its self-made cyclone.

Around the world millions of fascinated TV viewers experienced the stomach-knotting thrill.

On board, three men and one woman felt the smooth but invincible thrust as the reusable craft arced over on its back and angled away from Vandenberg Air Force Base on California's west coast. Four computers aimed it over the open

Pacific and toward the perpetual ice of the South Pole. In less than two hours it would sweep north over the ice cap at the top of the world, beginning the first polar orbital mission of its kind.

Explosive charges blasted away the boosters, and from the spacious cabin the flight commander reported:

"Launch Control, this is Shuttle Charlotte. We have booster separation. Thirty-one miles downrange and all is A-okay."

Commander James Carlyle, in a white NASA jumpsuit, had experienced the awesome power on three earlier launches. This time, though, the forty-two-year-old former 747 pilot gripped his chair arms as if he were beneath a dentist's drill.

While his concentration shifted over fourteen hundred instruments all around him and the three nine-inch TV screens that showed he was on course, his mind repeated the words he had spoken to his wife before boarding: *This is the last time, I promise.*

After all, how often could a man ride a rocket into orbit and live to see his grandchildren? Regardless of how careful and lucky the National Aeronautics and Space Administration's engineers could be, sooner or later they were going to have a failure.

He didn't want to be aboard when that occurred.

"Shuttle Charlotte, this is Control. We have booster parachutes in sight and tugs moving in to collect them. You have a 'go' for separation of main external tank in four minutes, fifty-one seconds. Do you copy?"

"Roger, Control. Main tank separation in"—he checked the instrument board digital clock—"in four minutes, forty-five seconds."

"How's Charlie doing?" the Launch Control director from Vandenberg asked.

"Too busy fighting off these lotharios to get anything done," Charlotte Von Kamp answered. It was in her honor that the shuttle had been renamed by the President of the United States.

In the seat directly behind Commander Carlyle, the young female scientist gripped the arms of her seat just as hard as he did.

Dr. Charlotte Von Kamp was a pert twenty-eight-year-old

scientist with a cute face and short brown hair. She made the flight historic—the first American woman in space.

To her right in the second rear seat sat her technician, Arnold Dumas, a handsome black man half again her age. Together they were charged with putting the ship's main payload—a new space telescope—into orbit.

Alex Bunyan, another three-time veteran of trucking scientists and their gear into orbit, rode in the copilot's seat. Unlike his commander, Alex Bunyan had no intention of quitting the space program.

Being an astronaut gave the young bachelor celebrity status, a boost for his social life.

"Ever made out in zero gravity?" he whispered in Charlotte's ear.

He saw her frown, then reconsider. "Kinky," she said. "A real historical first."

"That a promise?"

"Charlotte," Commander Carlyle interrupted, "Launch Control is asking—"

"Oh, yes, fine. Everything's fine."

"Okay, Vandenberg." James Carlyle returned to business. "We have main engine shutdown."

"Go for separation."

Outside, the large tank broke away from the ship. As big as a fifteen-story farm silo, it would crack up and melt in the friction-caused heat as it reentered the earth's atmosphere.

When it had drifted away, nothing remained except the orbiter, with its cockpit on one level, its living quarters one deck down, and the sixty-foot cargo area between the cockpit and the tail/wing combination. The shuttle looked like a stubby jumbo jetliner. But instead of several large engines, it would now use forty-four small rockets for maneuvering.

"Firing for orbital velocity," Carlyle reported. "Velocity seventeen thousand, five hundred. We're up to speed."

"Orbital altitudes as estimated. Sixty nautical miles to an apogee of one hundred fifty," copilot Alex Bunyan contributed.

"Going for circular orbit," Commander Carlyle said.

Again small rockets blasted for a matter of seconds, and the computer replied reassuringly. They were in a circular orbit.

"Everything still okay," Commander Carlyle reported.

"Right on, shuttle. This is Launch Control turning you over to Mission Control."

The radio crackled, and the launch team at Vandenberg, its job finished, turned the shuttle over to the NASA center in Houston, Texas.

At his display console, launch director Russell Gardner leaned back in his chair and thought of his young wife's cute little ass. Tonight it was all his. The shuttle was launched, his job done. No more overtime. The rest of the mission was controlled from Texas.

"Russ!" a young technician called, breaking off Gardner's concentration just as his imagination was sliding his hand down between two mounds of young flesh. "Unauthorized personnel on the field."

"What?"

"Unauthorized personnel . . ."

Gardner stood up, staring at a large screen display of the now empty gantry that had so recently held the giant spacecraft. "Well, I'll be as hairy as a whore's cunt!" He wasn't even aware of his exclamation. He was pointing at a man running through the still steaming launch area toward an open part of the complex. "He can't do that. How the hell? Somebody get him."

"Security! Security!" a voice barked.

A raucous klaxon blared. Air Force guards carrying automatic rifles dogtrotted onto the field, their sergeant shouting at the figure in the open.

"Halt! Halt! Damn it, halt or we'll fire."

The launch director was out of the control room, moving with half his crew toward the lone figure. The hills still echoed with the roar of the powerful engines. The air was heavy with the stench of burned chemicals. And from out of the rolling blast cloud, a yellow helicopter was dropping toward the figure.

"Hold your fire," the sergeant yelled as he saw his men aiming toward the clattering chopper. "It's got to be one of ours."

But even as he finished his sentence, he saw the cargo door slide open and a heavy-caliber weapon swing toward his troops.

The muzzle flared. The loud pops punctured the clatter of the copter blades. Tracers drew a line from one side of his squad to the other. Slugs chipped at the sidewalk, adjusted for range, and began moving toward the Air Force guards.

An airman dropped his weapon and grabbed his groin. Blood splashed from between his legs. Another was set spinning like a top. A third seemed to change his mind and flew backwards, his head hanging by tendons before he hit the pavement.

The heavy weapon swung across again as the chopper came close enough to the ground for a pickup of the running man. Another swath by the machine gun and three more airmen went down, hands and fingers chopped away as if by a butcher's cleaver. The interloper was half through the open cargo door before the first Air Force guards realized they had carried no bullets in the chambers of their weapons: orders from some safety-conscious idiot.

Pulling a weapon from beneath a fresh corpse, Gardner put the bloody butt against his cheek, rammed a bullet home, and fired at the helicopter's fuel tank just as the bigger gun was moving toward him.

A balloon of red and yellow flame, metal parts, and human limbs exploded ten feet off the concrete. Scrap and burning material peaked, then began settling to the ground.

A moment later the launch area lay silent. Technicians and reporters all stood frozen, staring at the burning wreckage. The wounded were bent over, not yet feeling the pain. Most were as still as death.

"What in the name of God was that?" a reporter asked.

Launch director Russell Gardner shook his head. "I don't know. What the fuck would anybody want to . . ." He stopped, shaking his head. It didn't make sense.

"Shuttle Charlotte," a voice said from Houston. "This is Mission Control. Do you read me?"

"Loud and clear, Mission Control. We're all yours."

"All right, take ten while we check telemetry data."

"Okay, Mission Control, we're going out for coffee." James Carlyle released a latch and swiveled his chair around to face his passengers.

"Bridge anyone?" he asked calmly.

"No, but I'll go below and fix that coffee," copilot Alex Bunyan offered. He released his safety harness and pulled himself up. He floated over Charlotte Von Kamp's head. "Care to give a dumb bachelor a hand, Doctor?"

"I'm not going down. . . . Oh, well, why not." She too released the safety belt and pushed lightly to take her up and over. She followed Bunyan, knowing he was leering happily.

The brazen chauvinist, she thought. He thinks every girl's hot for his body. But to set a world first . . .

She hoped they would have time.

Sooner or later, she realized, somewhere in the flight they would make time. Alex Bunyan wasn't one to let astronomy stand in the way of a real science like biology.

In Houston, Mission Control director Fred Yarkin ran his gaze across the displays and consoles spread before him.

The vast room was strangely empty of technicians. There were only a dozen men and women at various TV-like display consoles, but he could have handled the project with three assistants.

Actually, there were more reporters and television network people beyond the glass wall to his back than there were workers in the control room.

From the stances of the men and women working with him, Fred Yarkin could see tension easing its grip on shoulders all up and down the line.

The shoulders, he thought sometimes, gave him as much information as all the expensive electronics that linked his console to the stream of data being received by his staff.

"We have verification of orbit," he confirmed for his staff.

He took the headset from his ears and welcomed the freedom from the pressure of soft plastic against his temples. All his words, and those from Vandenburg and the shuttle craft itself, were broadcast to the entire room by wall speakers unless he restricted the system, but Yarkin preferred the intimacy of the headset. He could hear the telltale pitches of voice better with all the surrounding noise eliminated.

A space flight should have become routine for Fred Yarkin

long ago. He had directed so many. To date he had never directed a fatal failure, yet a manned launch always left him bathed in perspiration as it did now.

"Mr. Yarkin."

He heard his name and jerked around as an aide handed him a special telephone. He took it and said, "Yarkin here."

"This is Vandenberg, Fred. Just had the damnedest thing. A gunfight around the gantry."

"Who is this? Wait." A messenger had urgently nudged his shoulder. His counterpart in California was trying to talk to him simultaneously from the telephone, but the balding Yarkin opened the envelope.

The messenger was from the top brass at NASA.

Extracting a sheet of paper, he read the words, expecting congratulations from his superiors, possibly the President.

"Bomb in Shuttle Charlotte fuel cell," he read. "Do not attempt landing until situation corrected."

"Oh, my God!" Yarkin groaned.

Chapter 2

NOTHING overpowered the din of slot machines on the casino floor. Mechanical arms snapped like broken pieces of wood. Coins clanked as they were dropped into perpetually open mouths. The money was sucked in faster than mackerel consume anchovies during a feeding frenzy. Quarters fell into the bottom metal troughs with a clatter, a ringing of bells, and a flashing of colorful lights.

"Cocktails, anyone?" Girls in short skirts and low-cut tops moved among customers at the roulette, blackjack, and crap tables.

"Forty-two, ten, six," the voice of the keno announcer said in a bored monotone.

"See your three and raise you three more," Steve Crown said in the relative quiet of the casino's poker corner.

He slid his six white chips across the green-felt-covered table into the center pyramid. To his left his opponents began turning over their up cards, leaving only an attractive blonde in her early thirties and one elderly woman nervously peeking at her two hidden cardboards.

"Gotta let you have it, sonny," the old lady said as she backed off. "And I know you're bluffin' sure'n I knowed when my husband had more in his hands than cards and chips when he'd been out all night."

"Sorry, granny."

The attention shifted to the blonde. She was the showgirl type, a little more makeup than necessary, a hopeful look in her eyes. But virginal too—or at least it hadn't been long since she'd lost it.

Pathetically, she looked at her cards and the two chips in front of her.

"You want to call, miss?" the house dealer asked.

"Yes, I . . ." Her sky-blue eyes considered the two chips she had in front of her. "I really ought to raise."

The dealer was patient. "Sorry, miss. It's table stakes. You can see him with what you got on the table. There's nobody else left."

Steve reached for his extra chip, then withdrew his hand sharply. A room key had come flying from her end of the table and bounced off his knuckles.

"And raise you the maximum, mister," she said in a desperate voice.

"Can't allow that, miss," the dealer said.

He went for the key, but Steve's hand had folded over his.

"Call," he said, pushing out a stack of new chips into the pot.

The worried dealer glanced at the pit boss, who grinned and shook his head when he saw it was Steve Crown at the table.

The dealer announced, "Pot's right. Here they come, down and dirty."

Steve leaned closer. Nearing thirty years old, he was tall—

well above six feet. He was a lean hundred and ninety-five pounds, good-looking if a woman liked the macho type with a black mustache and a slightly Slavic look.

The last card slid across the table to him but he left it facedown.

"The lady's in, Mr. Crown," the dealer said. "And only you two left. That makes it a showdown."

The girl flipped over her cards. "High flush," she said. "I had it going in."

"Two pair," Steve announced, adding, "going in."

His first six cards flipped queens and fives.

Every eye went to the remaining and decisive card. He still had not turned it over.

The girl looked up hopefully, pathetically.

He flipped it.

A five of clubs.

"Full house beats the flush." The dealer swept the chips toward Steve.

The pretty virgin face grew angry. "Damn you. Goddamn you."

She grabbed for the key, but Steve already had it. "Cash me in, dealer," he said. "I'll be back."

Then he was around the table, catching her arm as she started through the gate in the railing that fenced off the poker players.

"You didn't have to look at that card," she was saying as he hurried her toward the elevators. "You could have been a gentleman and let me win." They started up to the floor number on the key. "You could see I was broke. Desperate."

They entered the upper hall with him smiling and her still talking. "All I needed was one winning hand."

The key slipped in a door and he pushed her inside.

"Look," she said, "you can't collect a gambling debt. Especially this one."

"What's your name?" he asked her as he pushed her to the bed and began unbuttoning his shirt.

"Edie. . . . I'll yell 'rape.' I'll . . ."

He stopped. "Oh?"

"Yes." She reached for the phone. "Look, I'll pay you someway. Not this."

"All right." He sat on the bed beside her.

"What are you going to do?"

"Collect. Just tell me if you change your mind."

In one motion, he pulled her facedown across his lap, held her in position handily with an elbow, and used both hands to slide her skirt and slip up her bare legs. She wore no panty hose in the Vegas heat, and what she did wear beneath was sheer and bikini style.

"What are you . . .? No . . . you can't . . . that's not fair." She yelped as he pulled her panties down and began to slap the less suntanned portions of her exposed anatomy.

"Thought you had a sure thing," he said as he spanked, not brutally, just smart slaps that stung and left little angry red areas. "A sucker," he said.

"No, honest, ow, not so hard. Please!"

"If you needed money, I'd have given you a mint. I just don't like being conned."

"Ouch, not there," she cried as he included her upper legs in the punishment. "It'll show."

"Draw a winner and make the sucker bet the maximum while he's looking down your boobs. Right?"

"Ow, I was desperate." She kicked, her legs interfering with his swatting.

"Feet down or I'll go for your hairbrush."

"No. All right, all right," she cried.

"All right, what?"

"I give up. You win. Ow. I'll pay off."

"How?" He kept spanking.

"You know how."

"No, I kind of like this."

"That's not fair."

Still he hadn't stopped. Then he realized she was no longer struggling. She wasn't lying still, but she wasn't trying to escape, either. Instead she was letting him spank while she crawled forward and began squirming, her lower belly and the place between her legs massaging his manhood as it strained to rise through his shorts and trousers.

For a few seconds longer he tried to hold off, then he rolled with her. She was partway on the bed, face up, feet on the floor, grinning at him, spread legs waiting as he ripped off his trousers. She rose high enough to help him.

He still wore a shirt and sport coat.

But it was the giant Wildey .45 magnum automatic in its concealable pancake shoulder holster that slipped forward and cracked her against the nose.

"My God, you're Mafia," she shrieked.

He laughed and shrugged off the gun, holster, and jacket. Everything fell to the floor behind him.

"Tell me about it later," she cried as she pulled him toward her.

"Much later."

He gave her little time, plunging into her quicker than usual.

She wasn't virgin. From the first, her hips thrust forward to meet him. He'd never been bashful about how he was hung, but she couldn't seem to get enough. Somewhere in the turmoil she fell to the floor. Their feet tangled under the bed. He raised his head and cracked the bottom of the table and she was hunched up against the leg to some piece of furniture, but there was no stopping either of them until they climaxed nearly together.

Still their fury continued, and he remembered asking, "You like that? The prelims on the bed, I mean?"

"Hell, no. It hurt," she protested between moaning. "You big chauvinistic pig. But God . . . you got hard and I . . . and I . . . Oh, fuck, someone's at the door."

"Room service," Steve answered.

"Steve. Steve Crown," the voice was calling from outside. "You in there?"

"No. What the hell would I be doing here? It's not mine." He hadn't missed a stroke.

The door opened. The girl rose on her elbow, tipped her head to one side, and looked around at Roy Borden, top engineer at Crown General Corporation. He was neither as tall nor quite as good-looking as his friend Steve. His hair wasn't as dark, either.

"Oh, Roy, nice you could drop in," Steve said. "This is Edie. Edie . . . ah. Ah. Well, anyway, this is Edie what's-her-name."

Neither had moved.

"Yes. Yes. That's right." She began to squirm free.

"Your grandfather called," Roy said solemnly. "It's another panic."

"You know what you can go do to yourself about dear old grandfather's panics, don't you, Roy, old buddy? I mean, just watch Edie and me and—"

"Now!" Roy said firmly. "It's allowance time."

"Aw, shit, Roy," Steve groaned. "Not again."

Edie picked up her clothes. "Allowance? You're still on an allowance?"

"A million dollars a year. Hardly keeps him in jelly beans." Usually serious, Roy could never smile as easily as Steve, his card-playing, woman-chasing buddy.

"Damn, Roy, I'm on a winning streak."

The protest went unheeded. Roy was heading for the door.

Steve dressed furiously, kissed Edie on the cheek, and ran after Roy, still buttoning his shirt.

"So what's the emergency this time?"

They had reached the outside of the casino, where signs lit hotel row to daylight brightness and traffic rolled bumper to bumper, pouring in and out of the darkness that surrounded the desert city for a hundred miles in any direction.

A cab waited against a background of glittering fountains, and Steve was hustled in, complaining about his clothes.

"Everything's in my suite," he argued.

Roy tapped the driver on the shoulder and dismissed the luggage problem with a promise to have it sent along later.

"So what's such a big rush?" Steve wanted to know.

The question went unanswered until they were alone in the passenger compartment of a company-owned Learjet rushing down the runway between parallel rows of lights.

"The shuttle's in trouble," Roy finally said.

"The space shuttle?"

Roy gave him a "What else?" type look and said, "I was on my way back from Vandenberg when I got the call from your grandfather."

Steve thought of Adam Crown, his sole surviving relative. The silver-haired former Bolshevik controlled Crown General

Corporation with an authoritarian hand that left no meaning to his grandson's title of vice-president. Steve had neither office nor desk at the company's San Diego headquarters.

The weapons and advanced technology produced by the vast firm were Adam Crown's penance for the atrocities he had directly and indirectly committed during his Communist days in Russia. And as if his weaponry weren't enough contribution to his adopted land, he had developed Counter Force. His second obsession, Counter Force was a tiny, private CIA with none of its larger counterpart's restrictions and taboos.

Since it was financed and staffed entirely by Crown, it was one covert-action group that could be called upon without bureaucratic restraints. It could be used anytime by the President, the secretaries of state and defense, plus the chief of the CIA. No one else even knew it existed.

"Did Crown have a big part in building the shuttle?" Steve asked. His knowledge of company business was almost nil.

"Negative," Roy replied. "But there was some kind of bizarre fracas at Vanderberg—a guy trying to escape right after the launch. Then NASA in Houston got a threatening note."

"Saying there's a bomb aboard?" Steve said skeptically.

"Yes."

"Hell, if the government starts taking every bomb threat seriously . . ."

"I happen to think it's true."

Steve turned curious. His friend was knowledgeable enough to know the odds. If Roy Borden said there was a bomb aboard, then there was.

"Shit," he muttered. He thought of the three men and one woman aboard the shuttle. He knew them all personally. He could imagine them outwardly ignoring the fear. But it was there, inside them, eating at their strength and control. He knew. He had been afraid a lot in his life, and like them, he rarely dared show it. "Who's working on it? The FBI?"

"Undoubtedly. I know NASA and the contractors have begun a plans search to pin down places where a bomb could be hidden. There's not much waste space aboard the orbiter. And Army munitions experts are being called in to suggest what kind of explosive and what type of detonator system might be used. They're trying to identify the bodies at Vandenberg, of course, assuming both situations are connected. But the bomb part is hush-hush. I'm not sure the astronauts know what they're riding with yet."

"And what am I supposed to do?"

"Get the shuttle down safely, I suppose."

"But the shuttle's—"

"—a hundred and thirty-eight miles straight up," Roy said dryly. "You're tall. Take care of it, will you?"

Chapter 3

ADAM Crown sat at the long table in the secret conference room at his San Diego mansion and called out to the tall, attractive brunette.

"Vodka," he demanded.

Usually a staunch female liberationist, Tanya Horton brought hors d'oeuvres into the room. Stopping at the built-in bar, she added a bottle of vodka and a single shot glass before placing everything in front of the sixty-nine-year-old man.

"Pickled cucumbers? Scallions?" he asked.

"And herring and smoked salmon and—"

A buzzer sounded. The stiffly erect old man glanced at a closed-circuit TV screen and identified his grandson and Roy

Borden waiting in the passageway outside. He pushed a button beneath the edge of the table.

Adam Crown, a cross between a stocky Russian peasant and an American business executive, wore a hand-tailored suit, a white shirt with a stiff collar, and a conservative tie. His hair was silver gray, his nose straight, his blue eyes locking on anyone who interested him.

As Steve and Roy entered, he kept his lips hard and thin beneath his bushy gray mustache. He rarely greeted anyone.

Tanya Horton followed his example. Only slightly past thirty, she had some of Adam's mannerisms. The sight of the handsome Steve, though, gave her a brief and foolish schoolgirl flutter, her typical response when she saw him after a long absence.

Sometimes she thought she was in love with him, but her more pragmatic side squelched sentimentality beneath an avalanche of reason. He had too many women: he was a playboy; he went through large segments of his life with no greater goal than the next game or party.

In between play times, he was a tough, heartless vigilante. The contrast never ceased to amaze and confuse her. Which was the real Steve Crown?

And he was reckless. Eventually he would get himself killed. When it happened, she wanted to have as few emotional strings between them as possible.

"The new space shuttle may have a bomb aboard," Adam announced without preliminaries.

He pushed another button beneath the table, and, as Steve and Roy sat down, a heavily accented voice spoke from a wall speaker.

"Bomb in Shuttle Charlotte fuel cells. Do not attempt landing until situation corrected."

"A German accent," Steve said.

"The voice was recorded automatically," Tanya explained.

Steve made a pyramid by placing the fingers of both hands together. The overwhelming urge inside him to counter any cruel, evil force started to bury his fun-loving, playboy side. "That's all you have to go on? A phone call?"

"No. The message was placed to an unlisted and restricted

code-room number at the Space Flight Center. Also, the caller knows that even the smallest bomb in the fuel cell system could cause the mixing of hydrogen and oxygen and other chemicals."

Steve nodded. "Causing a secondary explosion."

"Precisely," Roy agreed.

Adam said, "We have another factor: the voice is familiar to several people involved in the space program."

"Including you?" Tanya asked.

"Yes. That's where we became involved. NASA guessed I might recognize the voice. And I do."

Steve was impatient. "Well, who the hell is it?"

"I can't remember. Neither can the others. The mind rules the person. Man is the ass in the harness of the brain. The harder we try to remember, the more determined the head becomes to keep us from looking back at the cart."

Tanya cut off his philosophizing. "Have all of you who recognize the voice hold a conference call. Determine when you worked together. Discuss common denominators that involve German scientists."

"The German rocket specialists brought here following the end of World War II?" Steve said. "Could the connection have gone back that far?"

"Yes, yes," Adam nodded.

"Narrow the field," Tanya continued. "Find recordings of men you consider possibilities and match voice prints."

"Brilliant," Adam said.

"Have the astronauts aboard the shuttle been informed of the threat?" Steve asked.

"They will be," his grandfather replied. "Not the public yet, of course. But the crew must search the craft."

Steve thought about the dangers aboard a manned spacecraft. The crew was in such a hostile environment, the circumstances of their possible death so terrifying. They could bake to death from increasing heat or die the slow torture of a failing air supply.

And any chance of actually helping them was so remote.

In a way they were as helpless as children—more so: children could run.

Then he thought of an angle others might overlook. It was

the way he worked. He went after the remote possibilities, leaving the more promising leads to the official experts.

"Play the recording for the crew."

"Why?" Roy said.

"Because the threat might have been made by a friend of an astronaut—as a joke or in an attempt to help."

Adam Crown poured himself a shot of vodka and drank it in one gulp, then cooled his throat with a bite of pickled herring. He was not particularly fond of his grandson when he came up with ideas that he had overlooked.

"And you're using the wrong term," Steve said. "That wasn't a threatening call. It was a warning. The caller might be attempting to avoid a catastrophe."

Adam Crown puzzled. A warning? He was not comfortable with the semantics. It sounded like a threat to him. But then terrorists often called to announce they had planted a bomb in a given building.

Steve rose and started for the door.

"Where are you going?" Adam asked.

"Houston."

"To the space center?"

"Yes."

Adam became touchy about his authority. "I have not designated this as a Counter Force endeavor. Nor has any of our four contacts in the government requested Counter Force assistance."

"Do you have any objections to my sniffing around the space center to see if there is something we can do?" he asked.

Adam goaded him. "I prefer you stay here, play errand boy to Tanya's idea about voice prints."

Roy Borden sensed a family feud brewing. "Errand boy" was a trigger term to Steve Crown's occasionally explosive temper. He interceded. "Steve can go to Houston with me. I want to see if I can help determine where a bomb would have to be placed to achieve a secondary explosion."

"You think that someone could get a bomb aboard a spacecraft in spite of all the inspection processes?" Steve remained skeptical.

Roy was certain. "Absolutely. Every inspection is another

opportunity to place a device aboard. The cells were undoubtedly inspected, X-rayed, heat tested, put on vibrators, and pawed by experts. During all that, a small charge could have been inserted in a number of places."

Steve stayed at the door.

Thoughtfully he said, "There's a girl aboard the shuttle, you know."

"An ex-girl friend?" Tanya asked sarcastically.

Steve grinned. "No. But she is kind of cute."

"Here we go again," she said. "Super stud to the rescue."

"Why don't you get lost in space, Tanya? See if some super stud comes to your rescue."

"The situation is serious." Adam Crown grew peevish. "If a madman placed a bomb aboard the craft, we not only lose four lives, we will also have to recognize that the security of the space program is easy to penetrate. If another nation is involved, we face an even more explosive situation. And finally a loss of life might sour Congress on further funding of the shuttle program."

"Four lives are in danger," Steve said. "That's enough for me. Roy and I will be using one of the company jets."

"Be careful," Tanya warned. "I'm afraid this goes far beyond a single kook."

Chapter 4

ABOARD the space shuttle, giant doors extending the length of the cargo compartment had been opened shortly after orbit was attained. The opening exposed the entire tightly packed hold, venting the buildup of heat.

The cargo was diversified. Besides the telescope to be placed over the South Pole, the freight included TV-network satellites, plus "getaway specials." The specials were various-sized canisters. In each one, a private company or scientific agency had placed chemicals or devices to test in space. One $3,000 canister even contained a solar research project by a group of high school kids.

The freight also concealed the latest Air Force attempt to place a missile interceptor into orbit. The constant fear of a holocaust might eventually ease if the missile-destroyer test model could be successfully parked in the sky.

All projects would be lifted from the hold by a thin fifty-foot mechanical arm.

Operated from within the ship with TV cameras providing vision, the robot arm had already lifted one container away. Outside the vacated area, Commander Carlyle in his bulky space suit had worked two panels off the hold's metal decking. He tried to ignore the infinite emptiness around him. If the little drive rockets on his backpack failed, he could die out there, ever so slowly.

The rest of the crew waited inside, but they knew.

The bomb scare had been reported to them on a scrambler line. For once, NASA's Mission Control was lying to the vast television audience.

"No use," James Carlyle reported solemnly by radio. "I can't see a thing. If there is a bomb, it's well hidden."

Inside, Arnold Dumas reported from the lower deck. "Nothing here either, Commander. Nothing I can reach."

"Roger. I'm returning to airlock."

On the flight deck, a calm Alex Bunyan had drawn Charlotte Von Kamp to him in a playful embrace. In the weightlessness they bumped noses hard. He kissed her, and they floated into a position with their heads to the floor.

"Alex, we could be in danger," she said.

"You are. I synchronized our sleep schedules."

"You did what?"

"You have to sleep with someone, babe." Alex grinned.

"Not in the same bed."

"I won't fasten my belt. Maybe I'll just float over to your bunk."

She squirmed loose, pushing Alex hard enough to send him thumping against the opposite bulkhead as Commander Carlyle came in from the airlock. He looked at both of them, expecting signs of strain or impending panic. Instead he saw the blush of embarrassment.

"Damn," Charlotte said. "I hope Mission Control doesn't call us down early."

A cool, collected woman, Carlyle thought. Personally he'd

have preferred to scrub the flight and aim for the runway at Vandenberg. If there was a bomb aboard, he'd like to test the threat now and get it over with.

"You all right?" he asked her. To reassure himself, perhaps. Play the macho role and allay his own fears.

"Of course."

A green light flashed in front of James Carlyle, and he checked with his copilot.

"Pressurization okay, Alex?"

"Roger, Commander."

Carlyle watched while Arnold Dumas floated up into the cabin before he tipped his head toward a wall mike and looked into a TV camera, well aware that he was being watched thousands of miles away in Houston. At the moment they were coming in over Australia.

"Mission Control, this is Shuttle Charlotte going to scrambler."

Fred Yarkin, the Mission Control director, responded instantly. "Affirmative, Charlotte, go to scrambler frequency."

James Carlyle changed frequencies with a degree of regret. The American space program had been generally so open. He disliked what the scrambler meant. They were keeping the truth from the people who paid the bills.

"Mission Control, this is Shuttle Charlotte on scrambler. Do you copy?"

"Roger, Charlotte. We copy. What did you find?"

"Everything negative, Control. If there is anything aboard that shouldn't be, we can't find it."

"Then you discount the call?" Fred Yarkin asked.

The commander looked about, searching the faces of his flight officer and his two passengers. They could all hear exactly what he heard coming over the wall speaker. He had a consensus without asking.

"Negative, Control. We didn't find anything. That doesn't mean an unauthorized device couldn't be stashed down there in all that piping."

"Do you request abort?"

Again James Carlyle searched the faces. While the decision was his, their lives were on the line too.

"Negative," he said reluctantly.

The speaker crackled nervously for a time before the voice from earth came through again.

"Then we're going for a complete mission, Shuttle Charlotte, since the warning advised against landing. We may extend mission to maximum duration if we think the extra time might be helpful."

"Roger, Control. We'll proceed with planned schedule." Commander Carlyle saw the smile appear on Charlotte Von Kamp's face. The plucky woman was actually looking forward to extending her stay in space.

If only she knew, he mused. Going for a maximum flight meant pressing their luck. Their food and water supply would be depleted before they came down. But being hungry and thirsty for a few days was nothing compared to the discomfort they would experience from the contaminated air they would be breathing during their last few hours.

In the end, if they misjudged their oxygen supply by as much as five minutes they could suffer permanent brain damage. A six to ten minute miscalculation—a jammed escape hatch even after they reached the ground—and they'd be dead.

He'd been through the experiment during training. The fouled oxygen they would be breathing during their last hours would strangle him with claustrophobia. He felt the walls closing in on him just thinking about what lay ahead.

Face it, he told himself. You've been afraid since the beginning. Since you first stepped into a spacecraft simulator. Damn fool, what were you trying to prove? Should have gotten out of the program long ago. Found a nice desk to fly.

"Roger, Houston." He spoke while he could still control his tone. "We'll bring running calculations to confirm maximum flight time. Do you want us to continue search?"

"No," Fred Yarkin replied. "But stand by. We have request from higher authority. Somebody wants you to listen to a recording of the caller's voice."

The space commander didn't understand the purpose. "What do we want to hear that crank for? You already told us the contents."

Arnold Dumas laughed. "I'll probably recognize my wife's

voice after all that flight insurance she had me take out."

His companions smiled and then sobered again as the scratchy recording played over the speaker.

"Bomb in Shuttle Charlotte fuel cells. Do not attempt landing until situation corrected."

"Nope," Arnold said. "That's not my old lady."

"Play it again, Control."

Carlyle couldn't hear clearly every word in the heavily accented sentences, but he felt an inner rage flaming in his guts.

The voice returned, louder and clearer.

"Bomb in Shuttle Charlotte fuel cells. Do not attempt landing until situation corrected."

James Carlyle heard one of his people speak, but it took him a second to realize who had reacted to the warning.

It was Charlotte Von Kamp.

What was it she had said?

"Father?"

Carlyle turned to face her. So did Arnold and Alex.

None seemed to believe what they had heard.

She recognized the voice, the caller who had threatened them all with an explosive, fiery death.

The call had come from her father.

Chapter 5

THE business jet sat down at Houston airport and taxied to the far side from the main terminal. Roy Borden had climbed from the copilot seat and was opening the main compartment door.

Before Steve Crown had shut down the twin power plants, a mechanic in a jumpsuit ran toward them from a small office. He carried a cordless telephone and made a circular motion with his index finger above his head.

"He wants you to keep the engines on," Roy called to Steve.

"Mr. Crown." The mechanic pushed past Roy and thrust the phone into the cockpit. "Urgent call from San Diego," he said.

"Thanks," Steve replied, closing the cabin door for privacy.

He knew who was on the other end of the line before he heard the terse, irritating greeting.

"Boy, that you?"

"Yeah, Gramps, what do you want?"

"Go to Miami immediately." The order was typical. Adam Crown rarely requested anything. He ordered.

"You go to Miami," Steve retorted. "I'm stopping at the space center."

"Roy goes to the center. There, brains must run the jackass computers. In Miami . . ." Adam Crown cast about for words. "You will do. So go. Fast."

"Look," Steve argued. "You dragged me from an all-night poker game, had me fly to San Diego, now Houston. If you think I'm going to fly to Miami without a copilot . . ."

"Go. If you are too tired to fly, why kill some poor copilot, too?"

"And fuel?"

"You have enough."

"How do you know?"

"Someone will tell me if I am wrong," the old man said.

"Shit! What's in Miami?" Steve said.

"We have identified the man who called in the warning. Eric Von Kamp." Adam Crown was reading from something. "Born 1917, Germany. Rocket expert at Peenemude. Captured by American troops April 1945. Came to the U.S. later the same year."

"Von Kamp . . . the girl on the shuttle . . ."

"His daughter. As soon as I heard the name, I knew the voice. Others in the space program remember Von Kamp too."

"Was he involved in the shuttle program."

"He worked on earlier spacecraft, so he has contacts."

"What else do you have on him?" Steve asked. "Anything to explain why he'd place such a call?"

"No. Go to Miami." Adam Crown read off an address. "Try to get there before the FBI. Talk to Von Kamp."

"Why don't you just call him?"

"Give the old respect and they will give you wisdom. Don't you think I called already? He doesn't answer his phone."

"All right."

Steve hung up the extension phone, opened the cabin door, and handed it back to the mechanic.

Steve shouted to Roy. "Gotta follow a lead Adam came up with. Call him. See if you can catch up with me."

Roy nodded and closed the door after himself. He was standing beside a waiting car when Steve had clearance from the tower and began moving the small jet into line between the towering 747s and DC-10s.

Rushing down the runway, he fought drowsiness. He still had hours of flying ahead, alone, but the prospect of work would keep him awake.

The two FBI agents parked their car several blocks down, then walked through the humid evening to the address Steve Crown had been given by his grandfather.

Steve parked his rented Cadillac nearby and cursed for having missed an opportunity to see Eric Von Kamp before the authorities got to him. He didn't think he stood a chance, but he decided to try for a few words with the former Nazi before the plodding agents took Von Kamp in for questioning.

The night was moonlit, but the house was on a rectangular man-made island shaded with thick-foliaged trees rather than tufted palms. The island, like so many others in the Miami area, had been formed with silt dredged from the once swampy land behind Miami Beach. It was reached by a series of bridges that connected six of the identical islands.

A street ran between rows of walled estates, each backed on brackish water with piers poking out with the regularity of a picket fence. Only the size of the boats varied. They ran from ski boats to sizable power yachts.

For a former Nazi, Eric Von Kamp had done well in defeat.

While the two agents figured an approach to the Moorish-style house behind a high iron fence, Steve moved in closer.

He knew the two agents, although he could recall neither man's name. He had worked with them once several years before. They were no more alert now than they had been then, and he climbed the fence unnoticed while they approached the gate.

In a crouch, he ran along a stone wall separating the Von

Kamp mansion from its neighbor. From the water, he walked toward the house while the FBI men were still waiting at the gate.

"You. You in there?" he heard one of them call. "We're FBI. Open up."

Steve couldn't tell whom they thought they were calling to. The two-story stucco house was well lit—even its patios and porches. Yet he could see no one through the wrought-iron grating that covered every first-floor window.

He pulled the magnum that he had brought along, ready for the watchdogs he expected.

It was that kind of house. One built for security.

But then so were the others on the islands. From adjoining mansions Dobermans and chows were barking, snarling, and leaping against the wall as he ran along it. One of the vicious animals could thrust his paws over the rim. With one extra-high leap he could scramble over to sink his fangs into Steve's face or throat.

A moment later Steve knew why the Von Kamp house was not similarily protected. He stumbled over a lump softer than dirt or stone. He knelt and felt the short fur of a Doberman. The body was sticky with blood, and the head felt mashed. It was the first of two dead dogs, large monsters probably trained to kill. Their training hadn't saved them.

How about himself, Steve wondered.

Wiping his hands on the grass, Steve thought about the dead animals.

Immediately the entire spacecraft scare took on a more believable color.

Death—of man or beast—underscored a grim fact.

Neither he nor the government was dealing with a mere crank call. At a Las Vegas gaming table he would have raised to the limit on a bet that there truly was a bomb aboard Shuttle Charlotte. He'd also bet that the shoot-out at Vandenberg was part of the same deadly scheme.

And as he ran toward a side entrance, crouched so that the bushes would conceal him from the FBI agents, his mind rushed ahead to what awaited him inside.

Chapter 6

A protective moat of floodlights surrounded the house, the white beams giving the building the cold look of a prison. The light was dimmer than daylight, but it made all the lines of the house more distinct.

Steve crouched, gun in hand, then sprinted across the lighted strip to the side entrance of the house. He flattened against the stucco wall.

From the front of the house he could hear the two FBI men climbing the fence. He doubted they had a warrant, and he wondered how far they would go to interview Von Kamp.

He got a response in the form of a gunshot.

The muffled crack came from inside the house.

Instinctively Steve thought it was aimed at him, and he burst in through the side entrance, startled to find it unlocked. He heard the two agents out front shouting at each other to take cover.

"Get down!"

"Behind the tree!"

There was another shot, then a third, and more shouting.

"Cover me."

"You, inside the house. We're FBI agents. Hold your fire."

Another shot defied them.

Inside, Steve entered a laundry room with a washer, a dryer, hampers, and shelves where fresh linens were supposed to be folded and stored. But the bedding and towels had all been dumped on the floor.

From the laundry he moved into a brightly lit kitchen. It too was in disarray, all cabinet doors open, pots and pans on the floor along with broken dishes. Before he entered the dining room, he knew the house had been searched.

And from the sounds of more shots and two men speaking Spanish in another room, he could tell the FBI men were still pinned down in front.

"Donde va?" one of the men inside shouted.

"Voy al bote!"

"No . . . primero pegamos fuego a la casa."

Fuego? Steve searched his meager Spanish vocabulary. *Fuego*. Fire. They were going to set fire to the house.

"Christ!" Steve said aloud.

What the hell was going on? A bomb aboard a spacecraft, a shoot-out at Vandenberg, and a warning phone call from the father of one astronaut. Now this. Dead guard dogs. Spanish-speaking men. Setting fire to the house.

And where was Von Kamp? Had the Latins killed him?

Stopping them became his prime concern. They represented terrorism and tyranny in all the forms he hated. The beasts of the world always had the guns and the power. They struck at the weak, the unarmed, and the unsuspecting. He got satisfaction when that kind of terrorist—under any kind of banner—came up against him. He gave the bastards a shock they never expected.

Positive that was the kind of people who were in the house,

he ran down a short corridor and flung open the door to the room the shots had come from.

He leaped into a spacious living room done in a Spanish style. He spun to the left as one of two figures at the shattered front window whirled and fired. The bullet dug into the casing above Steve's head.

Steve snapped off a shot, using instinct shooting. The thin Latin face splattered into a painting of garbage.

Steve Crown was momentarily stunned.

It had been a girl. Twenty-two, twenty-three. Small boned. The olive skin of a Latin American. Not beautiful. She might have been pretty if she had tried, but in that second he had seen only hate. The all-encompassing hate of the professional terrorist.

He knew the kind. They fought for any cause. And if captured after a kill, they glared at the captors who would deny their passion for slaughter.

But a girl.

She flew back under the impact of the heavy slug, bounced off the wall, then slumped to one side on the floor. She still held the gun in her hand.

What had she found worth dying for? he wondered.

He almost wondered too long. There were still two men in the room. One he had seen at the window with the girl, and one he had almost failed to notice by the door.

The man at the door had turned and fired.

The slug missed by inches. The crack of the bullet passing so close jabbed Steve into action. He started to leap back through the door, then realized that's exactly what his unknown enemy expected. In fact, the Latin-looking guy had fired through the open doorway, assuming that's where his target would be. But it wasn't.

Steve leaped into the living room instead, hit the floor on his shoulder, rolled toward a couch, and then reversed his roll just as two slugs poked through the upholstery and jabbed holes in the floor where he had been for a fraction of a second. This time he continued through the door, kicked it closed behind him with his foot, and sprang into another room he could enter from the hall.

Inside the room, a combination library and den, he latched the door and stepped away. He waited. No one pursued him, and in a moment he surveyed the room. It too had been searched. The contents of a desk were scattered on the floor and the books torn from their shelves.

Then he smelled smoke and heard the ghostly rustle of fire from beyond the hall.

"Damn," he said.

This would be the only room he would have a chance to search.

Outside, the FBI men were shouting.

". . .place on fire."

"Cover me."

"Get around the back. Watch the boat dock."

Steve waded through the scattered papers.

The room had been ransacked, no doubt about that. But there was something out of kilter. He wasted a moment trying to decide what troubled him.

Then he knew.

The upholstered furniture had not been sliced so the stuffing and springs could be searched. Pictures on the wall had not been moved to reveal a possible safe. And an expensive chess set lay undisturbed. Someone had been looking for objects that were not likely to be well hidden.

Steve coughed. The smoke was coming in under the door. He took one of the scatter rugs that covered parts of the beautiful parquet floor and started to stuff it in the crack where gray-brown spirals of smoke snaked in. But before he could put the rug in place, fangs of fire penetrated the room.

Like most fires in homes with aged wood floors, the flames were spreading like wine spilled on a polished tabletop.

The door reached the flash point and began to blaze.

It was like being tossed into a cage with a hungry tiger. The only other exit was through the window, and the sounds of shooting proved that one of the FBI men had reached the front patio just outside the study window.

Trapped, Steve held his position, knowing he probably wouldn't get a chance to surrender to the government agents. With only two of them as witnesses, they'd go the safe route—

kill at first sight. Taking prisoners was dangerous.

They'd shoot him the second he jumped out.

The alternative was allowing himself to be burned alive.

With the decision obvious, he cherished the moments before he went out shooting.

He scanned the room, intending to get an overall impression. Instead he fixed on a table. The top was filled with framed photographs. Family pictures. One was faintly familiar.

Von Kamp, he decided. He could not recall when he had met the man, but he knew the face. No doubt they had met during one of the rare occasions when Steve was doing work for Crown General Corporation.

Ignoring the flames now covering one entire wall and burning across the floor like fire advancing through a forest, he went to the table and took out the photo. He folded it to put it in his pocket.

He recognized a second photo, too.

Charlotte Von Kamp, the space scientist, the latter-day Amelia Earhart. Her picture had been on TV lately.

In the photo, she was still in her teens.

Across it was an inscription he almost failed to notice.

"To Daddy. Love, Carlotta."

Carlotta? Was that her real name? he wondered.

Carlotta. Latin-sounding, like the voices of the men so zealously guarding the house. A connection? Must be.

There were several pictures of another woman, lined up in a chronological sequence, showing her growth from a young woman to a matron. Probably Von Kamp's wife. The woman had blond good looks and Charlotte's eyes and mouth.

"Doesn't tell me much," he said, evaluating the tabletop.

The fire was coming for the table and had consumed enough of the walls, floor, and furnishings to roar like a wounded animal that had regained strength to threaten.

Determined, Steve practiced something his grandfather had taught him. He looked at the table with a different question in mind. What didn't he see?

"Silence in a forest," Adam had said once, "can tell you as much about the presence of wolves as a flash of the fur."

There was something missing.

The pictures were symmetrically placed, and Steve noticed gaps in the positioning of the frames.

At least two pictures had been removed.

Again, curious.

But he had no opportunity to contemplate the meaning behind the photographs' removal. Smoke was filling the room, making his eyes water and forcing him to stoop in order to get down where the air was not yet contaminated.

The electricity went off, and the room was illuminated only by the fire, which cast eerie shadows and contrasted them with areas of brilliantly lit spears of light.

Using his last minutes, he cast about in the strewn papers. He found nothing except a checkbook showing a balance under a thousand dollars.

He saw the desk calendar and thumbed through it.

Simultaneously he realized the fire had outfoxed him and had surrounded the window and started to build a wall of flames between him and the exit. He couldn't escape that way.

He stuffed the desk calendar in his pocket. They were always potential evidence, and he had gained nothing else.

Grabbing a rug and wrapping it around his head and torso, he took bounding steps through the fire and crashed through the door back into the hall. It was a desperation route.

It was a tunnel of flames, and he plunged down it toward the kitchen, holding his breath. He meant to hurl straight through and on outside, yelling, but at the kitchen he slammed into another figure, one of the Latin gunmen still inside.

Their impact knocked them apart, and they lurched against the stand-up freezer-refrigerator, one on either side. The exit was across the room. The other man peered around to see whom he had bumped. Eyes steaming with tears, Steve fired.

An ear flew off the other man's head. He yelled and cursed.

But they were both in the same predicament: each holding a gun around the refrigerator front, peeking out, waiting for a shot, and the room burning around them. The fluorescent light fixtures fell to the floor. Cabinet doors caught fire, feeding hungrily on the layered lacquer. The liquor supply blazed.

Thinking quickly, Steve ducked a burning piece of rubble falling from the ceiling, picked it up where he could, and tossed it over the refrigerator. The man screamed, and Steve snatched up a barbecue fork that had rolled to the floor. The two points were glowing red, the handle too hot to hold for more than seconds.

Steve looked up just in time to see his opponent, the shoulders of his jacket in flames and his hair burned away. The man had climbed to a counter, then to the refrigerator top. He attempted to get his gun into position for a killing shot straight down through the brain.

Steve speared upward with the fork. It pierced the man's right eye and continued straight up into the brain. The cry was from hell itself. It wasn't Steve's style. It was a dirty kill, a sadist's kill. But he hadn't had time to think.

The man on top of the refrigerator fired, then dropped his weapon, his reflexes pulling his hands toward his eye. He was alive but in agony.

Steve dove across the room, and rolled into the yard.

"Don't shoot," he yelled.

He expected an FBI man to come at him with a gun, but he discovered himself alone. Not questioning his good luck, he sprinted across the yard toward the front fence. As he ran out the gate he glimpsed two pistols firing at a figure on the pier. In the moonlight the form seemed to be lifted off its feet, carried a short distance, and dumped in the water.

Evidently the wounded Latin had failed to make good his escape.

Sirens wailed. Lights went on in houses along either side of the street. People in nightclothes appeared at the gates.

"What's happening?" a man shouted at Steve.

"A shooting," he replied.

"Everybody get back inside." A take-charge type had emerged and was running down the center of the street. He provided the distraction Steve needed to get in his car. He got it started and headed for the bridge.

He floored the accelerator, and the car leaped ahead, laying rubber on the takeoff and again at the corner. When he saw the flashing lights coming, Steve swung to the curb and parked. With the Cadillac's lights still out, he doubted the police would notice him. While responding to a shooting report, they'd be more conscious of anyone making a quick retreat.

When they had turned onto the street that ran parallel to the length of the island, Steve sped along the street again, his lights still out. Too late he saw the wet figure pulling itself up from the water. The man from the house! Steve hit the brakes. He wanted the suspect alive, but again timing tripped him up. Arms outstretched, the Latin ran straight toward the car. The fender hardly grazed him, a brushing motion that wouldn't even dent the car, but it sent the wounded man spinning against the concrete railing. His head cracked loud enough to be heard inside the car.

"Damn fool," Steve swore.

He considered stopping, then knew it was useless. If the guy wasn't dead, he would be soon, and Steve Crown would be tied up in court for weeks.

He kept driving.

Maybe nobody would even know he had been in the house.

Forcing himself to a comfortable speed, he turned on his lights and drove to the mainland. A fire truck racing to the blaze nearly smashed him at the corner, but he ran up over the curb and was back in his proper lane driving at a moderate rate when he passed two more police cars.

A glance back at the burning house, and for him the incident was closed, he hoped.

The two FBI agents had never seen him. The man and woman in the house were dead. The one on the bridge was ready to join his cohorts soon.

Who they were and what they were doing in Von Kamp's house were questions the authorities could pursue better than he.

As exhausted as he was, he drove up to Fort Lauderdale before he checked into a cheap hotel with a sleepy night clerk who couldn't care less what his guest looked like. Most of them—couples—stayed only a few hours anyway.

Carrying his luggage, Steve went to his room, showered, and stretched out on the bed, naked.

If he closed his eyes, he wouldn't wake for hours.

But curiosity nudged him again, and he turned on the TV set to an all-news station.

Nothing so far about the fire and shoot-out. He wasn't surprised. And according to the newscaster, the space shuttle was still in a flawless flight, although the reporters were still speculating wildly on what had happened at Vandenberg following the launch.

Idly, Steve thumbed through the desk calendar he had brought from the house. It was the only thing he had to show for nearly losing his life.

There were few notations on the calendar. Most concerned luncheons and dental appointments. On the pages marking the days before the launch of the shuttle, there was a countdown penciled in with numbers, a natural thing for a proud father to plot.

And on the last day, there were several phone numbers. He tried the first two and got no answer.

Probably business phones, he told himself.

Toward the bottom of the page he came to another set of numbers. Not the usual seven digits, this one was ten figures long, three of the numbers written below the rest.

An area code, he decided.

Fighting off sleep, he dialed the long-distance number and leaned back to wait, not knowing what to expect.

Two rings and then a woman's recorded voice. "The number you have reached is not in service at this time, and there is—"

He hung up, flung the desk calendar to the bottom of the bed, and closed his eyes.

Nothing. He had nearly been killed and had nothing to show for it except more questions than he had started with.

A thought yanked him alert, and he took up the calendar again. This time he dialed locally, using only the top seven numbers.

It rang a dozen times before a male with a slight Spanish accent answered.

"Aerolineas Argentinas. May I help you, please?"

The response startled Steve, and when he didn't respond, the clerk resorted to Spanish.

"Ola, habla usted español o ingles?"

"English," Steve replied.

"Ah, may I help you then?"

Steve had his gaze focused on the number, and he tried to imagine himself making the notation.

"My name is . . . Von Kamp. Eric Von Kamp."

"Sí, señor. Do you wish to make a reservation?"

"Yes. No. I believe I already have a reservation."

"You don't know, sir?"

"My travel agent . . . very careless. So I wanted to check."

"And what flight were you supposed to be booked on?"

Steve looked at the calendar pad again.

"Sir?" The reservation clerk was growing impatient.

The three digits beneath the phone number stood out.

"Flight 714," he said hopefully.

"For tonight, sir?"

Again Steve bluffed. "That's just it. I'm not certain when I was booked for—yesterday, today, or tomorrow."

"One moment, please."

As he waited, Steve studied the calendar pad.

If it had been important, it would have been removed, like the two photographs from the table in Von Kamp's library.

No, he corrected himself. The woman and two men had intended to burn the house. They could reasonably expect the fire to wipe out any moderately important information.

But the pictures. They were in a different category.

Shit, he thought. He knew damned little about where he was heading.

"Yes, Mr. Von Kamp. Now I remember. You were booked on Flight 714 to Buenos Aires for tonight."

Steve swung his feet over the edge of the bed. "Good. I'll be right down."

"But, sir. Flight 714 left on schedule two hours ago. I recall. You were escorted by those two men and girl. You . . ."

Missed him! The only lead he had, and Steve had missed Von Kamp by two hours. And the former rocket engineer had been escorted to the airport—possibly by the three people who had burned his house later. Christ! he thought. Had the Latin trio urged or compelled Von Kamp to leave the country?

"Was there some mix-up, sir?" the clerk asked.

Steve seized on the chance. "Hell, yes. You let somebody else use my ticket."

"Sir?"

"How fast can you get me to Buenos Aires?"

"Not until tomorrow morning. But I believe another airline has a flight leaving in an hour or two."

"Get me on it."

"Yes, sir. I can do that for you. I can confirm you on that flight." He gave the details. "Please come to the airport as quickly as possible."

Steve hung up and dialed long distance immediately. A moment later he had his grandfather on the line.

"Anything I don't know yet?" Steve demanded crisply.

Adam seemed to leave the phone for a moment, and when he returned, he started to tell his grandson about the fire at Von Kamp's Miami home.

"Skip that. I was there. Anything else?"

"You were there?"

"Look," Steve snapped. "I'm fighting a flight time. I have to get to the airport. I have my passport, but I'll need a visa waiting for me in Argentina. Arrange it. Is there anything I should know?"

"No," Adam conceded. "And, yes, I will arrange the visa."

"Then I want Roy to join me in Buenos Aires."

"No. We need him at Houston. And what is this nonsense about Argentina?"

"I think Eric Von Kamp is headed there on his own or perhaps against his will. The fire might have been a way to conceal clues to his whereabouts."

"Think? You need more than a hunch. What could Argentina have to do with our space shuttle? That country has been plagued by political instability, authoritarian government, and fanaticism—in the street and in high places—most of this century."

Steve searched his memory. "I thought the military junta was going to allow free elections soon."

He knew Argentina. He thought about it as a beautiful South American country lying like an arrowhead that poked 2,300 miles down the Atlantic coast from Brazil almost to Antarctica.

It probably had thirty million people, mostly of European extraction, a majority of whom lived in Buenos Aires now that the pampas, the land of the gaucho, was being mechanized.

"Still," Adam argued, "what do Argentina elections have to do with our space shuttle?"

Steve ignored him. "Have Tanya meet me there instead. Let's see. At the Hotel California. And send a dossier on Von Kamp too. Everything including his family. Especially any Argentine connection he might have had. Plus I want more info on the shuttle. Orbital track, a complete list of emergency landing spots, a timetable of possible landings."

"You're issuing orders, boy. I run Counter Force. I am the rooster, you the chicken."

"Well, I plucked at least two turkeys for you tonight. So I'll crow whenever I damn well please."

"You killed? Why?"

Steve told Adam what had happened, concluding with, "So even an old man like you can help in a crisis."

"An old man! Before you were born, I..."

Steve stopped. He had joshed his grandfather enough. Neither had time to waste.

"Just get me the information. And a safe house in Buenos Aires in case I have to go to ground."

"There is no safe house."

"Get a CIA one then."

Adam scoffed at the espionage agency. "They're as impotent as a mule down there. The CIA isn't taking any chances of getting caught with their noses in Argentine politics."

"Damn!"

"But we have friends there. Señor Miguel Romonas Marcelo de Juárez. He looks after our interests. And Corpus Cristi."

"Who?"

"Corpus Cristi. They will meet you if they can."

Steve hung up the phone and looked at the gun in his belt. He'd have to get rid of that somewhere between the hotel and the airport. He was going to feel naked until he had another.

Chapter 7

ERIC Von Kamp had the walk of a proud, defiant man, the face of determination, the eyes of suspicion. Before he rose to leave Aerolineas Argentinas Flight 714, he waited until all but the wheelchair passengers had funneled down the parallel aisles to the exit.

Then he strode briskly toward the front of the plane where he bowed his head sharply to the stewardesses and steward.

"Adiós, señoritas y señores."

"*Adiós*," they replied politely.

His Germanic-accented Spanish was worse than his English, but there were social principles involved and memories of days when Argentina had supported Nazi Germany while America bombed his home into rubble. When his former enemies had decided his brain was useful, they had put him to work.

The old grudges were not as deeply buried as he had thought, and under different circumstances he would have had a more courteous greeting for the two men waiting for him outside the customs station in the bustling terminal.

"Señor Von Kamp?" The younger of the two men approached him after checking a picture small enough to fit in his palm. "*Permitame presentarme a mi mismo. Estoy Carlo Duarte.*"

Tall and strong, Carlo Duarte was in his early twenties with black hair and the devious look of a pickpocket in his eyes.

He waited for the importance of his surname to sink in. "*Un sobrino de Señora Evita Perón*," he said, thrusting his chest out with the pride of royalty.

Von Kamp was not impressed. Probably ten percent of Argentina claimed some relationship to Evita Perón, the long dead patron saint of the poor working classes. She and her husband lived on in the minds of fools like this one, who claimed to be her nephew.

"*Y esta es Jaime Paz.*"

The one called Jaime Paz looked stupid to Von Kamp. The eyes were vacant of thought, the cheeks sallow.

The Paz name was Latin, but he was undoubtedly a mestizo, a mixture of European and Indian ancestry. Unlike much of South America, Argentina had exterminated so many Indians, their blood line was not a factor except in the remote northern interior. The few blacks brought in during colonial days had so completely intermarried through the centuries that only a few thousand retained negroid characteristics.

So Argentina was European in appearance.

"*Descamisados*," Von Kamp said, refusing to hide his disgust as he referred to the two men's dress. While most men in the Buenos Aires terminal were in suits and ties, his two-man welcoming committee wore shirts with the sleeves rolled up above their elbows. They were the "shirtless ones," as many Argentina laborers called themselves. Rolled-up sleeves was enough for a man to be called a *descamisado*.

"Speak English," the man called Jaime ordered with a scowl. "Your Spanish is bad. And watch your words," he warned.

"Where are you taking me?" Eric Von Kamp asked as the two men guided him by the elbows toward the exit.

From the cool air conditioning of the terminal they stepped out into the stifling humidity of an Argentine summer day. Cabs and airport shuttle buses lined the curb, but a black Volkswagen station wagon came speeding down the open lane and braked to a stop. The driver leaped out, tossed the luggage in the rear, and had returned to the wheel before Duarte and Paz had Eric Von Kamp in the rear seat.

Jaime Paz had taken the seat beside the driver. Carlo Duarte sat next to their guest. The muzzle of a pistol poked the older man in the ribs.

Von Kamp looked down at it with disgust.

"You need a gun? Why? I came of my own free will," he said.

Duarte's response was muffled by the sudden sound of loud chanting. Von Kamp spotted the crowd and rolled down the window before his escorts could stop him.

The people lined the road. Several thousand were being shoved about and bullied by police in riot gear. Their identity was evident from their attire. Shirt sleeves rolled above the elbow. Even the women, greatly outnumbered by the men, wore long-sleeved blouses which they too could roll up their arms.

A tenth of the men were bare to the waist, the muscles of manual laborers bulging beneath dark olive skin.

"Perón! Perón! Puto o ladrón, queremos a Perón."

Son of a bitch or thief, we love Perón.

My God! Von Kamp thought. Juan Perón had been dead since '74, and yet the laboring class was still screaming the former dictator's name. It took him back to the heady days of his youth, when the brown shirt Nazis were demonstrating in the streets of Germany. Life had been exciting then.

When the crowd changed their booming chant, Von Kamp's face paled. The cry brought him back from his past.

"Resurjale ahorita!"

"Resurrect him now!" Carlo Duarte smirked. "You like that, Señor Von Kamp? Resurrect him. Juan Perón. Give the workers their fair power. Give us back our leader. You like?"

"No, he was a butcher."

"Never," Jaime shrieked. "Never our Perón kill. Before him, yes. After him, yes. Many die. But Perón, *no matanza*. And his wife, Evita—a saint in spite of what the church says."

"You are . . . how you say . . . *envidioso*. Envious. You prefer it was your Hitler we raise from the dead? No?" Duarte gloated.

Eric Von Kamp had no answer to the question. Juan Perón or Adolf Hitler. Which would he prefer to have raised from the grave?

Tanya Horton rode in first class for a change. Only the need to use an in-flight telephone persuaded her to go the extra expense, but she luxuriated in the comfort as the flight winged down across the Yucatán and the headwaters of the Amazon.

Now Tanya braced the phone between her shoulder and elbow while taking notes in rapid bursts of shorthand.

". . . a son?" Tanya was saying, her head turned slightly toward the window so her voice wouldn't carry. "Domingo. D-o-m-i-n-g-o." She wrote carefully in the book. "Any middle name or initial?"

Somewhere in Washington, through Adam Crown's influence, a clerk was assigned to assist Tanya. A platoon of researchers answered her flood of questions. Tanya had never been trained in forensic research, but then the entire government was usually at her disposal when Counter Force became involved in anything like the current bomb crisis.

"No. Just a nickname—Dom," a woman responded in the earphone. "Domingo, a rather strange name for the son of a German. Wait. Here's another point—Von Kamp's daughter. The girl aboard the shuttle. Her real name is Carlotta. She must have anglicized it. And here's the connection. Eric Von Kamp married a radio actress during World War II, a Maria Gallardo."

"An actress? Where?" Tanya probed.

"It doesn't say. All I have is Mr. Von Kamp's security file.

Let's see, his wife died in 1944, must have been just shortly after she gave birth to their son. He was born that same year. The girl is the daughter of a second wife, a woman he married in the states, also deceased."

"Did the second wife have a Latin name too?"

"No. Born Rockton, Illinois. Virginia Norton. Age twenty-two when she was married—quite an age difference between them. Probably agreed to call her daughter Carlotta because of her stepson's name. Died at the age of thirty-two of leukemia."

"Any security question marks on any of them?"

The response was fast. "None. Mr. Von Kamp was a Nazi, of course. But a war crimes inquiry cleared him before he came to this country. 'By choice,' it says here."

"What precisely does that mean?"

"Theoretically he had his choice: come to the States and work on our missile program or go over to the Communists. If the Reds had captured him, he might have worked for them. And the others. The second Mrs. Von Kamp, Domingo, Charlotte—all cleared repeatedly through the years. Not a hint of any Communist connection or inclination. The only trips any of them made out of the country were to Argentina. And those were business trips made by Domingo."

"What about the father and daughter?"

"I have no record of either traveling outside the U.S."

"And where do I reach Domingo Von Kamp?"

The phone was dormant for several minutes before the research expert in Washington returned.

"Last known address, California State Polytechnic College at San Luis Obispo. That's near Vandenberg Air Force Base. I wonder if he got to see his sister launched the other day."

"Check him out further for me, please. Fast."

"Certainly. Does this have anything to do with the shuttle? Is it in trouble or something?" The woman changed her mind. "I'm sorry. Never mind. I have no need to know."

"It's all right," Tanya lied. "The shuttle is doing fine. We're just concerned about Mr. Von Kamp. We're afraid he's been exposed to a toxic chemical and we're trying to track him down."

She replaced the instrument, finished her notes, then stared into space for a moment.

She had a hunch.

Darn, she was getting more like Steve with every assignment. Stick to facts, she advised herself. Forget silly hunches.

Yet she picked up the phone again and made connection with a land-based military exchange. Minutes later, a grouchy Adam Crown was on the other end of the line.

"Yah!" he said.

"Tanya, Mr. Crown."

"So?"

"I need you to get through to Charlotte Von Kamp aboard the space shuttle and ask her a question for me."

"For you? *I* am the big cheese! Are you getting like that boy, forgetting who asks the questions?"

"No, sir, but I can't get patched through from here."

"You're nibbling at my crazy grandson's hunch. We have no time for you to waste proving he is wrong."

"No, Mr. Crown. I think Steve is onto something."

"Of course. His hunches always lead somewhere, as straight to the point as a drunken peasant's plow. You think I sent you after him to make love in the field? I sent you to keep his mind on the mission."

"There is some Latin connection," Tanya said with conviction. "What it is, I'll be darned if I know."

"So what is it you want me—your new personal secretary—to ask this astronaut girl?"

"Ask her if her father ever visited Spain, Argentina, or any other Spanish-speaking country. If he did, get all the details. Ask what she knows about her father's first wife. You can call me in Buenos Aires. We desperately need a starting point."

"All right, I will get you your information, but do not expect me to get your coffee when you come to the office again."

Tanya hung up the phone and put it on the next seat.

From the window Buenos Aires appeared as a dark smudge on the horizon. The city was so clouded with pollution that it was impossible to make out the grid pattern of its street layout.

What lay below that threatened an American space shuttle?

she wondered. She could not fathom the connection, yet she knew there was a chain of circumstances that posed a threat—to the three men and one woman on the shuttle.

And to Steve Crown by now. To her, too.

She could sense the danger like a deer sniffing the breeze for a hunter's scent, but she could not figure from which direction the threat was approaching.

Chapter 8

AFTER midnight Corpus Cristi appeared at the Buenos Aires customs gate in slacks and a white blouse. She was small and slender with a sweet innocent face. Her hair was naturally blond, and she was still in her early twenties.

She carried a small purse, a mini-revolver inside with the lipstick and the other makeup. The gun could be concealed in her small hands, but the stainless steel cylinder held four rounds.

"Ah, Señor Crown, mi amigo," she said as she recognized Steve Crown. "I am Corpus Cristi, your guide."

Steve grinned. His grandfather must have goofed, assigning him a cute broad with adequate breasts and an appealing shape.

"Can we speak English, Corpus? Is that what people call you?" Steve asked when they reached the exit.

"Most of my friends call me Cristi."

Chattering effusively, she led her tired visitor past the taxis and buses that ran to the center of the city. "I was raised by Collas Indians. Spanish is foreign to me also."

"You speak English well enough."

"To survive. I was born in the province of Jujuy, where fathers still fill their pockets with resins from the yareta plant to assure their daughter will grow beautiful and healthy."

"Your father must have had large pockets." Steve measured her dimensions and approved of the design.

"My parents were Creoles, pure-blooded Spaniards born in Argentina. My real mother died giving me birth. My father . . . *poof*." She made a little explosive sound. "My Collas mother says I grew to be not tall because she did not rub enough sheep manure on my legs when I was slow to walk."

"She what?"

Cristi ignored the question. They had reached a black limousine with the windows heavily tinted except in front.

"It is true. My people still put a cricket in a child's mouth to bite his tongue if he is slow to talk."

"Does it work?"

"Does it work?" Corpus Cristi raised her hands over her head. "Some son of a bitch puts a cricket in your mouth, and you have nothing to say? Of course, it works."

"Señor Crown," a more cultured voice said from the car.

A hand with glove-leather smoothness and manicured nails reached through the open door to welcome Steve. He stooped and peered into the dim rear compartment.

"May I introduce myself? Miguel Romonas Marcelo de Juárez, honored to represent Crown General Corporation in Argentina."

The other end of the introduction was simpler.

"Steve Crown here."

Steve took the offered hand and started to slip into the rear seat beside his host until he noticed the thick, tinted glass that separated them from the chauffeur and the front, where Cristi was preparing to sit.

"There's room back here," Steve offered.

"Oh, no, señor."

Class consciousness, Steve guessed. Well, to hell with that.

"I am sure Señorita Cristi prefers . . . ," he said.

With no effort at appeasing the Latin class sensitivities, Steve eased the girl into the middle before testing the door latch to be certain it could be opened from inside. Only then did he take the right-hand position.

A pompous man, Miguel Marcelo pressed far to the left. "Señorita Cristi and I have just now met," he said.

They nodded at each other.

"A strange name, Corpus Cristi," Steve said.

"But you are not Indian," the girl replied. "My people, they don't read so good. What is there to read in a mud hut with a thatched roof? In a village with nothing but one store, where the barber, the dentist, and the doctor come once a month . . . sometimes."

"I still don't see . . ."

Miguel Marcelo explained. "How the Indians select names for their children? Quite ingenious, actually. If they cannot find a priest to baptize their newborn, the child receives 'the helping' water from whoever is present. And the family selects a name from whatever is available to read. A calendar, a map."

"I have a brother Holy Week, another called Revolution Day."

Her English improved intermittently.

"But what do Indians know? No more than how to track across the sea of pampas with no compass, no map. Only their instinct. You shame me by making me sit between two such fine gentlemen."

"Bullshit!" Steve said, squelching both of his greeters with the coarseness of his response. "Save the humility."

The driver turned onto Avenida 9 de Julio, the world's widest avenue—a block-wide expanse of cars flanked by tall, full-leafed trees and modern buildings plus the Teatro Colon, one of the world's greatest opera houses. Midway down the boulevard a traffic circle surrounded a monument built much like the memorial to George Washington in the States.

The European influence dominated Buenos Aires. There

were street cafés and expensive boutiques along either side. The sidewalks were teeming with people, and at crosswalks the pedestrians ran the gauntlet of racing cars.

The *porteños*, as the residents of the city called themselves, never seemed to sleep. At one A.M. hordes of people were drifting into theaters and restaurants.

"You're taking me out of my way to my hotel," he said.

"*Mi casa es su casa*," Miguel said graciously. "Please stay at my home."

"Thank you, no, Señor Marcelo," Steve responded. "I need to rest, then work." He used a telephone at his elbow to speak to the chauffeur. "Take me to the Hotel California, please."

"Don Miguel, please."

"I beg your pardon."

"Call me Don Miguel. It is the custom."

"Then call me Steve. Don Steve doesn't sound natural."

"Steve, then."

Corpus Cristi said, "Call me anything."

"You'll stay with me," Steve told her. "I assume you're on the payroll."

"Oh, yes, your company is most generous." She smiled.

"Then you will join me for dinner," Don Miguel said to Steve, deliberately leaving the girl out of the invitation.

Steve considered including Cristi on his own, then decided he had no right to interfere in the customs of the country that involved a man's home.

"Tomorrow evening?"

"But, of course. Ten o'clock, then. If you wish to meet with me at the office tomorrow . . ."

"No, give me a day to get acclimatized."

The car had stopped short of the hotel.

"Trouble," Don Miguel observed. "The fool Peronistas are putting up a fuss again. They have put their dead hero's name on the ballot."

The sidewalk in front of the hotel was crowded with a band of perhaps two hundred men in shirt sleeves scuffling with police who beat them with truncheons.

Like fish nibbling at the edge of a school of bait, the officers would pull a demonstrator from the edge of the group, crack his head with the clubs and, when he was down, kick his stomach and stomp on his face. The bloodied were left on the pavement while the officers went for fresh bait.

Both sides behaved at the animal level. The Peronists gathered together in a ball for a protection, and the police snapped at the bait fish even when their paddy wagons were full. Seals, Steve knew, would go on killing and tossing bonito around like toys after they had satisfied their hunger.

He would have helped, but which group deserved it?

"*Un, dos, tres, Perón otra vez,*" the crowd was chanting.

"The fools," Miguel remarked. "I fear they will make revolution again."

"It's been nearly thirty years since he and his wife Evita ruled the country, hasn't it?"

Steve recalled that Juan Perón had been a colonel who rose to power during the early forties and sided with Hitler and Mussolini until it was obvious the Fascists were going to lose. Perón had gained popular acclaim from the poor and the laboring masses when he and his charismatic wife had promised an improvement in the downtrodden's lot. They had delivered on many of those promises before they wrecked the economy.

Don Miguel replied, "He was legally president from 1946 to 1955 until the military exiled him after the death of his wife. When the military junta could not bring peace and stability to the country for eighteen years, the generals called him back in desperation. He served a year more before he died."

"And now?"

"Always it is the same when we attempt to have a free election. Turmoil. One president after another. Strikes. Work slowdowns. Financial chaos."

"The people are hungry," Corpus Cristi replied as the chauffeur reached the door. "The people pray for work."

"It is the Communists in the GRU that cause the hunger."

"What's the GRU?" Steve asked.

"The General Labor Confederation," Don Miguel explained. "The generals in the ruling junta outlawed it after Perón's death, but it is like a bad meal; it rises from the darkness long after it is finished, leaving a taste of bile in the mouth."

Steve had climbed from the limousine. Then so had Cristi.

A porter was collecting the suitcases. Cristi turned toward a side exit to the hotel before Steve had bidden Don Miguel farewell and stood staring at a battle near the main entrance.

"Why are they fighting over Perón?" he asked Cristi.

"Perón? They cheer because he will rise again."

"From the dead?"

"Yes. Somehow. It has been promised."

"Promised by whom?"

"It has been promised. That is all I know."

Crazy, Steve thought. What the hell was he doing in a country where it looked like the lid might blow at any minute while he was supposed to be saving a crew of astronauts?

More important. Why had Eric Von Kamp come here when he thought his own daughter was in imminent danger?

Chapter 9

OUTSIDE the hotel, Steve saw the demonstrator drive a knife into the belly of a uniformed officer and watched the policeman double over, dropping his nightstick. He yelled in Spanish, and his attacker withdrew his knife and made a break from the crowd.

Another police officer raised his Uzi automatic weapon. The fleeing protester darted a few yards directly at Steve Crown, then changed course, heading for a break between two parked cars at the curb in an attempt to reach the wide thoroughfare and the cover provided by its slowly moving traffic.

It was a problem of split seconds that left Steve wondering afterwards.

"*Pare usted!*" the police officer shouted.

Leaving no time for compliance with the command to stop, the officer fired the short-barrel Israeli machine gun from the hip. Nine-millimeter bullets chipped the sidewalk, missed the fleeing man, and kept coming at Steve Crown.

Corpus Cristi leaped sideways, hitting Steve with a shoulder. Cristi bounced off and out of the line of fire. Momentum knocked Steve to the concrete behind a stack of tumbling luggage. The remaining bullets in the 25-shot clip chewed at the suitcases and handbags.

Instinctively Steve rolled around the side of the building, rising in time to see another police officer step into Avenida 9 de Julio. His weapon had the stock extended, and he raised it to his shoulder for accuracy. He cut down the fleeing man with one short burst, chopping the demonstrator's body into chunks attached to the skeleton by flaps of flesh. His left hand was nearly torn from his wrist, his jaw was hit at the hinge point and ripped from the bone on one side. A leg was completely severed and left behind as the man made one final step.

There was more shooting. In the air, Steve thought, but from his concealed position, he couldn't be certain. He could hear the Peronists scattering.

Steve jumped up, intending to charge the first policeman to fire.

"That son of a bitch was aiming at me."

Corpus Cristi blocked him with her body. "No, he shoots at the Peronistas. Not you."

Steve flung his anger at his Argentine guide. "You, damn you. You practically knocked me into the line of fire."

Corpus Cristi shrugged. "Sorry, Don Steve. I try."

Steve cooled. He slapped his helper on the shoulder. "Could have got yourself shot in the process. Thanks anyway." He looked to the street, where the police were examining the body. Everything in Argentina was exaggerated. Monuments were ten times life-size. The presidential palace was a bawdy pink. The country was the Texas of South America, and apparently the police still played Wyatt Earp. "Did they have to kill the poor fool?"

"But, of course. The people have a demonstration. The police kill someone. Soon the people run out of demonstrators or the police run out of bullets. Then the election is over."

Steve frowned at the macabre sense of humor.

A bellman picked up the luggage and led them into the lobby. Hotel guests were emerging from behind chairs and other cover.

At the registration counter Steve tried to forget the incident. Argentine political squabbles were not his business.

A clerk greeted him, mentioned that the Crown General Corporation had made a second reservation for a Señorita Tanya Horton, and passed across a message that had been received.

They registered Corpus Cristi in still another room, then followed the bellman through the ornate lobby and rode the elevator to the third floor.

Handing his new guide a wad of money, Steve told her to furnish the room with liquor and snacks, then settled into a comfortable chair to read. The message baffled him until he decided it had been sent in response to questions by Tanya.

"Charlotte contacted. Recalls father mentioning trip in '44 to negotiate swap of Argentine beef for Nazi rocket technology. She recalls he met with the president, name Ramirez. Also met first wife, who died in Germany before the end of the war. Charlotte (real name Carlotta) has no information on her half brother Domingo."

Half brother? So Von Kamp had a Spanish wife and a son. Interesting.

His mind flashed a picture of a table in a burning room. Two photographs had been missing. A first wife? And a son?

Was it their pictures that had been taken? The son's picture surely should have been displayed with the others in Von Kamp's home. Maybe the Latin gunman had come to get Domingo Von Kamp's photo—or destroy it.

More important, did the pictures have anything to do with the space shuttle troubles?

"Domingo was aerospace engineer. Now teaching at CSPC," the message concluded. It was unsigned.

Steve stuffed the paper in his pocket, then relaxed on the bed.

He kept trying to reconstruct what had happened on the street. He had nearly been killed.

An unrelated accident? Of course.

"Why, of course?" He sat up straight. "Shit, that fucking trigger-happy cop could have been bribed to dust me."

"Señor?"

Corpus Cristi looked puzzled as she pushed open the door with her foot and entered, carrying a tray of liquor and snacks. She brought the tray to the bed and sat on the edge, smiling.

Steve asked, "Exactly how are you supposed to help me?"

Cristi spread her hands. "I do anything. I am your guide, your interpreter, your guard. I get things for you. Do things."

"Can you get us a couple of handguns unofficially?"

"Dos pistoles?" Her eyes glinted. It was the kind of request that carried with it the promise of rich rewards.

"Four," Steve said. "I have one friend joining me for certain. And a chance of a second coming down from the States."

"But, of course. There are always guns to be had in Argentina, although it is not the season."

"The season for what?"

"Revolution. Argentines do not attempt coups on Sundays or during the months for *vacaciones*. Naturally it will take—"

"—money." Steve finished the sentence for her.

"No, no, that is not what I intended to say. I am sure you will be generous. North Americans always are. I meant to say, it will take several hours to arrange."

"Good." Steve closed his eyes. He could use the break to sleep. But before Corpus Cristi could leave the room, another thought forced its way to the surface. "You know of an ex-president named Ramirez?"

"Yes."

"Any idea how I could get to see him?"

"It is easy. I take you to him anytime."

"Tonight?"

"Esta noche?" She frowned suspiciously. "As you wish."

Exhaustion overpowered Steve Crown's own suspicions. How could an apparently down and out Argentine girl arrange a meeting with an ex-president on the spur of the moment?

Later, he told himself, question her later. Right now sleep was more demanding than a bitchy wife. But before he'd given into it, Cristi set the tray aside and leaned over him, gently rubbing his leg.

"You're tired," she said. "No sleep, eh?" Her hand was on the inside of his leg, above the knee.

"Is this part of your job description?" he asked. She didn't know what he meant. "Never mind." He was tired, too tired to get it up, he was certain. But the idea of making love to one of his grandfather's aides was appealing. A cookie stolen from the jar has more sugar than one freely received, Adam Crown would have said. "Charge the old man double," he said, pulling her down to kiss.

"Charge? For this?" Cristi became incensed. She cursed in Spanish and aimed a slap at Steve's face.

"No, no, you misunderstood," he lied. Her anger eased, and he kissed her gently. Her lips were hot, her eyes sparkling.

No wonder his old grandfather liked traveling around the world, lining up people who would do anything without asking questions.

He pulled her on top of him. She was the last thing he needed right now. Rest, that's what he should be getting, but once he felt her try to pull away, indecisive about what she had started so soon, he was past turning back.

"No, it is a sin," she protested.

"To the old religion of the Collas?" he asked.

"No. I don't think so. But so soon we meet."

"But Collas—do they have good calendars?"

"No. You confuse me, Steve."

"Do Collas girls like this?" He unbuttoned her blouse and found no bra beneath. He kissed her between the small, smooth mounds, first one side, then the other. She moved, shifting until her nipple was in his mouth.

"There. Collas girls like that better."

"And this?" he said, his hands going down between her legs and rubbing gently through her slacks.

"*Sí. Sí.* How you know so much about Indians?"

"How about clothes?"

"No. Nobody likes clothes." She pulled away long enough to shuck herself of the blouse. Then she sat up on her knees and helped him remove his trousers. Their hands tangled as he went for the zipper at the side of her pants. Getting her naked was like wrestling in the mud. They both rolled and tossed and squirmed, trying to get the slacks down her legs. By then neither wanted to waste time on his shirt.

She stayed above him, impaling herself and then going wild. The bed creaked and groaned. Springs threatened to break. The headboard bent inward, but there was no stopping for either of them, and as he felt himself coming, Steve rolled over—still inside her—putting her below but keeping his weight off her tiny body, at the same time thrusting at her with all his strength.

Then it was over. Thirty or forty seconds of wild frenzy before they fell to either side and stared at the ceiling.

"Now you start me," she said. "You do every day or Corpus Cristi, she go crazy. Okay?"

"That's a promise," he said. "An oath. Every day." He closed his eyes, thinking, I haven't got time for sex. I haven't got time to sleep. People's lives depend on me. God knows what else. I haven't got time.

Steve closed his eyes.

When Cristi left, he didn't notice.

The Mercedes driven by Cristi, who talked to the car the way she might talk to a horse, pulled into the short driveway and stopped. A figure peered out of the shadows, then opened the gate and allowed the car to drive in.

The beams cleared a path through the darkness, but Steve Crown couldn't understand what he was seeing. The street was paved but abnormally narrow, the gutters were unusually clean for Buenos Aires, and the sidewalks were empty of people.

"Where are we?" he asked. They were passing through a section of stone mansions decorated with domes, spires, and porticos.

But the mansions were not full-size.

It was eerie, like stepping through a time warp in a science fiction novel. The elaborate mansions were three-quarter size.

Or had they entered an amusement park city?

He expected animated dolls—robots and kings and queens and knights in shining armor—to step from heavy, tarnished bronze doors ready to do battle with the uninvited intruders.

The walls, though, were real. Marble and granite. Doors of bronze and brass. Urns filled with real plants and flowers. There were no yards or gardens. The mansions abutted one another or even shared common walls. Few had windows on the street, not unusual in a Latin country where the wealthy and the middle class lived lavishly behind crude, whitewashed facades rather than rouse the dangerous envy of the masses. The few buildings that did have windows all had stained glass behind iron gratings.

Corpus Cristi finally answered his question,

"Recoleta," she said. She was astonished that Steve hadn't known where they would see the ex-president of Argentina.

"A cemetery," Steve groaned.

"Yes. Magnificent, isn't it?"

She stopped the car where two men in work clothes, each holding a large flashlight, waited on the sidewalk.

Hell, Steve thought. He should have known. A man old enough to be president in the forties was likely to be dead.

"Come, you meet the president." Cristi opened the car door.

Steve had changed his mind. "No, thanks."

His guide was hurt. "But, my friend, you ask. I arrange."

"I understand. I'll pay whatever's fair."

"Pay! Do you *norteamericanos* ever think of anything except money. It is an insult. In my country, we revere the dead."

"All right, all right." Steve climbed from the car.

As he approached the mausoleum entrance flanked by the two men with flashlights, Steve regretted leaving the guns behind in the hotel. Graveyards made him cautious.

So his hearing was particularly acute. He heard the rustling noise of many feet on the pavement before the other men noticed. But Cristi was quick to grasp the meaning of the sound.

"Peronistas," she whispered. "They come here most nights although it is forbidden."

Curious, Steve walked deeper into the web of narrow, paved alleys, along the row of ghostly mansions, mausoleums for thirteen former Argentine presidents and other prominent families with long patrician names. The names, etched deep in stone, accented the elitist attempt to carry their status with them into eternity.

In a country where the social position of the rich was demonstrated by the size of their houses, the magnificent tombs carried conspicuous consumption to the afterlife.

It was eerie. He was trying to save the lives of three men and a woman who were searching for the truth of science, and here he was, wandering around in the mystic snobbery of those who had sought to embalm their past.

He could almost believe that the dead were luring him away from his mission with sorcery and witchcraft.

Their tombs were awesome.

Each building strived to outdo the other with a taller spire or a more elaborate column, a more expensive monument or the most expensive kind of marble. Outside one stood the life-size bronze statue of a boxer in his dressing gown.

"The Bull," Corpus Cristi whispered with awe. "He knocked Jack Dempsey out of the ring."

There were generals on stone horses, too, and politicians addressing nonexistent crowds. There were healthy, living cyprus trees amid the chaos of marble and granite, yet the palaces of the dead were strange and bleak, with not a weed or a blade of grass even in the cracks in the pavement. "It is easier for the devil to get into heaven than for an Indian to get into Recoleta," Corpus Cristi whispered.

She restrained Steve with a gentle touch when they were close enough to a twist in the road to distinguish hushed voices mingled with the shuffling of slow-moving feet.

"No farther," she pleaded.

Steve looked around the corner. A hundred or more dark shapes lined up to enter a particularly opulent vault.

"So many," he observed.

"Tonight is special," she said. "This was why I get you in to see Ramirez tonight. The guards had already been bribed."

"It's the grave of Perón, isn't it?"

"Yes, and Santa Evita."

"I want to go in too."

"No, no. It is dangerous."

"I'll chance it."

"Then take off your jacket. Roll up your sleeves."

Steve removed his jacket and did as he was told before joining the end of the line of people shuffling toward the crypt patterned after Napoleon's tomb, topped by a giant statue of a workingman cut from Carrara marble.

Men held attack rifles across their chests, but no one prevented Steve from joining the line. He guessed they were not worrying about civilians but the soldiers of the military junta.

When he entered the tomb, its flowers stifled the air with a pleasant but heavy scent. Bronze scrolls on the walls listed the accomplishments of the former president and his wife. There were marble chairs for mourners and a chapel for prayers on behalf of the dead. A galaxy of candles burned in holders along one wall.

A magnificent marble staircase led to a basement room.

At the top Steve was stopped by a bone-thin face crusted with years of labor. The man checked Steve, then motioned him on.

It was then that Steve remembered reading about the grotesque travels of the dead Evita.

When she died, the generals had taken control of the country again and spirited her embalmed corpse away. For a decade and a half she had lain buried in an Italian grave under a false name. She had been brought home secretly years later and buried in her own family crypt, bought with money taken from the people during her husband's reign. Here she had remained, her corpse guarded until recently for fear her former disciples would show it as proof that they truly represented the political theology she so successfully promoted during her lifetime.

Continuing down the staircase with the few remaining mourners, Steve saw the two caskets at the bottom of the steps.

Juan Perón's coffin was ornately decorated in black and gold, its lid covered by a black shroud. On top of that was an elaborate sword and a staff of his high office.

Evita's was a masterpiece of the coffin maker's craft. More important, the lid was not shrouded. It was transparent—glass or plastic; Steve could not be certain in the poor light.

Dressed in a white gown, lying on a tufted white bed with her hands folded at her waist, she seemed to be sleeping.

Decades after death, embalmers' plastic left her lifelike.

There was only one flaw.

One finger had been broken off in the body's travels.

Then a man below spoke in Spanish, and with the other observers, Steve retreated up the stairs and into the night. Most of the people had spread out, and it took him some time to realize they were scattering themselves through the national pantheon to serve as lookouts.

"Please, let's leave." Corpus Cristi had come closer to tug at Steve's shirt sleeve. "You asked to see President Ramirez. Not this."

Steve was not certain what made his guide so nervous. She'd sneaked him into the cemetery, but she was terrified now that they were viewing the weird ceremony at the tomb of the Peróns.

Why?

He got his answer quickly.

So it could not be heard, a truck backed down the narrow street, its lights out, its motor off. Six or seven men were pushing it from the front. One man inside was steering. More preceded it, motioning with their hands to guide the driver.

Without a word, those in front held up their hands, palms forward to signal the driver to apply the brakes.

It came to a stop in front of the monument to the Peróns.

Quietly two men opened the rear doors of the empty truck.

"Please," Cristi begged.

Steve had no excuse for staying. He was on a vital mission, and he was wasting time watching some local ritual that was foreign to his thinking. But he could not draw himself away.

He had to know if he had guessed correctly about what was transpiring before him.

He was not surprised when minutes later the shadows of eight men, divided in two parallel lines, emerged from the tomb.

They were carrying one coffin: the transparent-top casket of Eva Perón. They slid it into the truck, then closed the door. Obviously they did not intend to take the strongman's body. Only his wife's.

Moving about with no more sound than an occasional click of metal or rustle of feet, they closed up the mausoleum and began pushing the truck toward an exit.

"They are going to succeed," Cristi said with marvel in her voice.

They—whoever they were—had the body of Evita.

They meant to use it as a flag of a new revolution. Of that, Steve was certain.

But how did that concern him? Were the grave-robbing and the shuttle flight connected, or was it a mere coincidence?

Chapter 10

STEVE Crown returned to the Mercedes, pausing when he saw khaki-colored trucks rounding the corner and moving slowly beneath a streetlight toward the entrance of Recoleta cemetery.

Cristi and her friends grasped the significance of the trucks before Steve did. He stared while the Latins leaped toward the car. They had it running and sweeping through the open gate before the soldiers could dismount from the rear of the trucks.

The night exploded.

The eerie quiet of the cemetery was blasted with a cacophony of grinding brakes, the shouts of soldiers, and the thump of boots hitting the pavement. Shots popped like a string of firecrackers tossed into a crowd. People screamed and called to each other.

The Peronists inside the cemetery reacted like a flock of startled bats. Those on foot hurled themselves in every direction away from the Perón tomb. They ran down alleys, climbed up the facades of tombs, and jumped from roof to roof.

Some soldiers clubbed skulls with their rifle butts; others held their weapons at port arms and tried to block those escaping without inflicting brutal blows.

Steve started back, deeper into the cemetery.

He couldn't afford to be caught with a bunch of ghoulish revolutionaries. The Argentine governing junta would roar.

CIA, they would shout.

And he couldn't blame the authorities if they accused him of consorting with the extremists. The generals, as totalitarian as their regime had been, were attempting to turn the government back to civilians. But these Peronists represented just another repressive political group that had tried to govern twice and nearly bankrupted the nation both times.

If an American were caught with the grave robbers, he'd be classed as supporting the enemy. What other possible explanation could he offer?

None.

While he retreated, he realized the army had the entire cemetery surrounded. They were taking some prisoners, netting them with the skill of experienced fishermen.

Only the unexpected disrupted the catch.

Crack. Crack. Crack. Crack. Crack.

Automatic rifle fire rattled from inside the cemetery.

The bullets ricocheted off stonework, whined past Steve's head, and cut down a soldier dogtrotting between the tombs.

Unexpectedly, the workers had a cross fire going.

Any sympathy the soldiers might have had for the people dissolved when they saw the wounded man, his right leg bent forward at the knee and bleeding profusely.

Officers shouted.

To Steve it sounded as if they were asking the men to hold their fire. Or maybe they were demanding a bloodbath. It didn't matter. The privates had opened fire, and he was in the center, bullets zinging at him from both directions.

He dropped as if he had been hit, exempting himself as a

target by falling on the pavement and faking an injured cry while he rolled to the curb. From there he dragged himself up the sidewalk and climbed a monument.

Rifle muzzle blasts were deadly fireflies, and bullets chipping marble blended with the cries of the wounded.

He wished he had a gun, then was glad he hadn't brought one. Whom would he shoot?

A soldier? Or the Peronists?

He didn't know which side was in the right, and it wasn't his fight. He had to concentrate on saving the astronauts. The coming revolution just made his task more difficult.

He had to get out of the cemetery. Escape.

That's what his mission required.

It was then he saw the men with weapons forming in front of the truck that carried the corpse of Evita Perón.

"*Vamos, Vamos,*" the driver shouted from the front.

There was more yelling and screaming, men raising their voices to mute the terrifying sound that exploded around them.

They were going for broke.

A flying squad of men with weapons was running and shooting in front of the truck. It was a suicide squad. Few if any of those on foot could hope to make it through the ring of soldiers.

That they would sacrifice themselves for a corpse appalled Steve, but their sacrifice offered him a chance to escape.

As the running shadow passed, firing wildly, he leaped to the road between the tombs. He came down running just behind the truck that served as a hearse. The truck was picking up speed.

He had one chance.

He grabbed for the rear door, both hands clutching for a handle. His right missed, but his left fingers folded around the metal grip. The speed of the truck yanked his arm, threatening to separate the wrist, elbow, and shoulder. The pain was excruciating. His legs dragged, quickly wearing through his trousers and burning his skin on the cement.

With his right hand, he pulled himself up and drew one side of the double doors open. He started to climb in.

A gun flashed in his eyes just after the truck lurched over a bump. Something hot laid a poker along his cheek.

"*Amigo, amigo,*" he yelled.

Instead of another bullet, a hand pulled him in. The truck bounced over a bump. Looking out from the darkness within, he could see what the driver had just run over.

Two of his own men.

"God," he said.

A rifle was thrust in his hands, and he recognized the test. Prove he was one of the Peronists. Shoot or die.

Through the open rear doors, he saw soldiers step into the street and raise their weapons. They were no more than black outlines. He fired. Once. Twice. Three times.

One man flew backwards. Another appeared to fall forward, but then the man next to Steve was firing too. So was somebody from the right front window of the cab. It might have been their bullets that had hit the soldiers, Steve told himself.

Then a piece of lead cut through his trousers and he no longer cared. He aimed to kill. If he was in the middle of someone else's war, he wasn't going to die without fighting.

The truck rammed something, and the grating impact tossed Steve back against the coffin. Yellow flames shot skyward behind him, and when he had righted himself, he looked into Evita Perón's face. For a second he imagined she had opened her eyes.

He saw what had happened when the driver swerved out of the gate and made a hard right turn.

An army truck was parked partially across the gate, leaving room for platoons of soldiers to pour into the cemetery. The hearse had smashed the side of the blockade vehicle, tipped it on its side, and split open its fuel tank. The gasoline had exploded, dousing half a dozen nearby soldiers with the burning liquid.

Screaming, the soldiers rolled in the street; their friends whipped off their coats and tried to smother the flames. With their attention diverted, they had allowed the hearse to wheel around the corner and speed away on a zigzag course that tossed the men in the back from side to side.

The fender grated against the tire; the vehicle was much like a horse gallantly trying to run on three legs. When a light showed Steve's face, the man sharing the rear with him recognized him as a stranger and swung his gun around for the kill.

Steve lunged forward, smashing his own rifle butt into the nose of the man who had just fought alongside him.

The crunching of bones reminded him of the sound of biting into dry toast. The gun butt came away bloody.

Tossing his own and the unconscious man's weapon into the street, Steve jumped after them.

He had no idea where he was. He only knew that he had to get away from the revolutionaries before the soldiers picked up the trail. And they were coming. He could hear the engines and see the headlights and trucks winding through the narrow street toward him.

Carrying one rifle, Steve darted down an alley. Even when he was several blocks from the military vehicles and the sound of more shooting, he continued to run.

When exhaustion caught up with him, he leaned against a wall, knocking over a garbage can that rolled down a slight incline.

A rat scurried across his foot.

He kicked at it blindly.

Inhaling deeply, he took inventory.

He was lost, but he was momentarily out of danger. He had money and he could say, *"Voy al Hotel California."* It would be enough Spanish to get him home if he could hail a cab.

Stumbling down the littered alley, he didn't come to the brightly lit city street he expected.

He was in slums. The buildings were old: dark stone structures, broken windows stuffed with rags, walls out of plumb. There were no streetlights. The few windows he could see into revealed cracked walls and bare bulbs hanging from the ceiling.

People on the crooked sidewalk sat on boxes or on the concrete, their backs against the walls. A few children moved about. Mostly the moonlit faces were old and scarred with disease or hollow from an inadequate diet.

The only cars to be seen were skeletons, stripped of wheels, bumpers, seats, and headlights that left their front ends looking like hollow-socket skulls. Farther on, the stone buildings gave way to shanties of scrap lumber and corrugated iron roofs.

Most had no doors, only shredded rags hung across the openings. Even this small claim to privacy was pulled aside in the muggy heat. Inside some hovels, he could see cooking fires, pouring half their smoke through holes in the ceilings and billowing the rest into a pall that fogged the upper third of the shacks.

In front of each hut squatted grotesque shapes.

No one seemed to notice him. Then a man stood and said something in Spanish. Steve spoke to him.

"Donde esta el centro commercial?" Steve struggled to make himself understood.

He got an obscene answer, punctuated with a bitter laugh.

More people rose. They stared at him. He turned around, feeling no fear, only sympathy for their poverty. *"Dispense usted,"* he said to no one in particular. *"No hablo bien su idioma.* Does anyone speak English?"

The people circled him. He spoke to one bony, misshapen figure that seemed the most pathetic among the lot.

"Puede guiarme por dinero?" he asked. He was certain he could hire a guide.

"*Sí,*" the cripple answered.

"Sí. Sí. Mi amigo." Three or four others tried to drown out the boy Steve had asked to guide him.

Then more were shouting. Hands were reaching out.

He realized his mistake. The poor ones had understood his Spanish perfectly. He was a foreigner. Lost. With money.

They came at him like animals.

For a moment pure sympathy restrained him. Then they began grabbing his clothes, some pleading and whimpering, some threatening. He took the change he had in his pocket and tossed it into their midst. Half dropped to their knees, searching frantically for the coins.

The more vicious wanted everything he had, including the gun.

They charged, and all his pity for them had to be discarded. He swung the rifle butt into a stomach, cracked another man's hand. Still they came at him.

And he glimpsed into the black hole of poverty that was behind the revolt he had seen starting tonight in the cemetery.

He had read about two and three hundred percent inflation rates in Argentina. Heard of food strikes and seen figures of huge unemployment in Latin American cities. He had even driven through the slums that ringed most capitals in the region.

But now hunger and poverty were rabid dogs coming after him.

He fired in the air. The crowd didn't stop.

He lowered the barrel and aimed at their legs. They slowed, then gambled and rushed him. He fired again, and a man screamed in pain.

The crowd stopped.

They let him back away and begin the nightlong search for his modern, air-conditioned hotel room with its built-in refrigerator and color TV.

Chapter 11

"YOU bitch!" Steve cursed as he approached his hotel room, where Corpus Cristi sat on the corridor floor, rising and smiling as he drew near.

"*Buenos días, Don Steve*. Such relief. You are alive."

"No thanks to you."

Cristi pretended to be confused. "What did I do, *amigo*?"

"You know damned well you drove off and left me." Steve fit his key into the lock.

"But I didn't see you in the dark and the excitement. And it was not I driving the Mercedes. Besides, I had to survive to tell your family that you were dead. No?"

"No, damn it." Steve opened the door and entered his room.

He stepped directly into Tanya Horton's path. She was on the way out, and he caught her arm at the elbow to prevent them from colliding any harder than they did.

"What the hell!" he uttered in surprise. He had known she was joining him, but she was still a shock.

"I was leaving you a note. Oh, my God." She saw the bruises and the streak burned into his face. "You're hurt!"

She saw Cristi then, and her sympathy paled.

Steve was quick to explain. "*That's* what my grandfather gave me for help. Corpus Cristi. Tanya Horton."

"Buenos días, señorita."

"Cristi!" Steve snapped. "Go do something. Make phone calls. Try to find Eric Von Kamp. Just get lost."

"You are angry, yes?"

"Hell, yes."

"You not break your promise. You start fire in Cristi, you—"

Steve swung the door closed on her face.

"What was all that about?" Tanya asked.

Steve feigned exhaustion. His hand covered his wound.

"What happened?" Tanya was sympathetic again as he groaned.

"I got in the middle of somebody else's revolution."

"Here, let me help you." She tugged him to the bathroom, stripped away his shirt, and washed the dirt from his wounds.

His feet killed him from a night of walking in search of a taxi, but the cool washcloth revived him, and he could not waste Tanya's rare touch of sympathy.

While she cleaned his wounds, he embraced her waist.

"You mind?" He referred to his hand sliding lower on her hips. With half-closed eyes, he played the battered-warrior role. "If I don't hang on . . . could pass out."

"We'd better get you a doctor."

"No, can't do that. The police might find out."

"Lean on me," she said. "I'll help you into bed."

He hooked his arm over her shoulders and let her support a little of his weight while his hand playfully touched her breast.

He forgot his wounds. He forgot the mission. Tanya and he had never really come close to going to bed together. Yet there were times—most of the time—when her lithe body aroused him.

But there was a problem. He had too many women. Tanya had no intention of being *e pluribus unum*, as the government printed on pennies. One composed of many. She didn't want to be part of any man's love affair with women in general. And they never got far enough for him to decide whether she was worth breaking relations with all the rest.

With her helping him into bed, though, he thought only of her. It was half game, half serious.

"My shoes," he said.

She undid the laces, then noticed his dirty trousers.

"You have shorts on, don't you?"

Wearily, eyes closed as if he were going to give in to the relief of unconsciousness, he whispered, "Yes."

He had to hold back a grin as she unfastened his pants and drew them off his legs. She tossed them on the floor and was about to cover him when he thought of a way to keep her with him.

"Telephone," he said. "Get Adam. Important."

Quite dramatic, he praised himself.

"You're hurt, Steve darling. You can't be thinking of work."

Had she really said "darling"? If she had, she had slipped the endearment in so quickly that he was left uncertain.

"Must," he said. "Get Adam."

"A doctor first."

"No. No time."

"All right, but you rest."

He couldn't bring himself to say, "Don't leave me." That would be putting Cherries Jubilee on top of Baked Alaska. Instead he held her wrist, forcing her to sit on the edge of the bed while she picked up the phone and put through the call.

Adam was on the phone in a matter of minutes.

"Hold it," Steve said of the phone, "so we both can hear."

Then he spoke to his grandfather. "Steve here."

"Playing, I suppose," the old man said.

Tanya came to Steve's defense. "He was nearly beaten to death last night." Her tone was peevish.

"Nearly shot, too. Grazed, in fact. I got your message to

Tanya," he said, looking up with baleful eyes to distract her from his stronger voice. He moved so she could lie beside him and listen easier.

"What happened?" Adam demanded.

"They're about to have a revolution here. The Peronists versus the military junta. Which side is Washington on?"

"Neither and both. Argentina is always plagued with discontent. But does it involve the shuttle?"

"Maybe. Or maybe it has nothing to do with us, except I don't like coincidences. Even little ones."

"Where do our interests connect with the Argentines'?"

"Item one. Von Kamp calls NASA, warns them his daughter is in danger, then flees to Argentina. Item two. He visited Buenos Aires in World War II. Negotiated with a president overthrown by Perón. Item three." Steve made certain Tanya could hear the next clearly, since the message from Adam had originally been meant for her. "Von Kamp married while he was here in '44."

"An Argentine actress," Adam added.

"You say he had a son by her."

"Yes. I have learned since, the son is fluent in Spanish and that he became an engineer only at his father's insistence. The boy—he is about forty now—was involved with NASA until recently, when he resigned to teach drama."

"Drama?" Steve started to sit up, but realized he was about to lose all he had gained with Tanya. He grimaced as if new pains struck him. "How does that fit in?"

Tanya said, "Not everything has to fit."

He clutched his burned face, and she leaned down to kiss it.

"There," she whispered. "Now it won't scar."

Her perfume was light yet sensual, like her body.

God, how he'd like to draw the drapes and close out the world—he and Tanya Horton, alone together, long enough to discover what they meant to each other. Maybe today, he thought.

"There is absolutely no hint of Communist involvement with any member of the family."

Steve's mind returned to work. "What about extreme rightists? Could Eric Von Kamp still harbor wild dreams about reviving the Nazi movement?"

"No," Adam said flatly. "He was not politically active under Hitler and has absolutely no connections with right-wingers in the States. And he hasn't been in Argentina since '44."

"And his son?"

"Nonpolitical too, as far as we know. And the sister in the shuttle—the same."

Steve kissed Tanya tenderly on the cheek.

"How about the U.S. government?" Steve asked. Beginning to doubt his own lead, he was casting about for another angle. "Has NASA or anyone else received any demands that have to be met before the shuttle is allowed to land safely?"

"No, just the one warning. The FBI is rechecking the lives of the other astronauts, too. The whole damned government is working the obvious possibilities. And getting nowhere."

"Then who the hell planted the bomb? Von Kamp himself?"

"He was a devoted father," Tanya said. She hardly noticed as Steve massaged her back. "What about the relationship between Charlotte and Domingo Von Kamp?"

Adam answered. "The girl assures us the family was close."

"Adam," Steve said thoughtfully. "Call the girl again. Ask her whose pictures were displayed in her father's study. Two pictures were missing when I went to his house."

"I will ask her."

Steve was digging into the obscure possibilities now. "Would they share a large estate if their father died?"

"Yes." Adam was ready with the answer. "Are you suggesting Domingo might be using the shuttle to kill his sister? That's a rather farfetched way to eliminate a co-beneficiary."

"Yeah," Steve agreed. "I'm running out of ideas. I hate to admit I came on a wild goose chase. So I keep coming back to Domingo. Has anyone seen or talked to him yet."

Adam said, "No. We called his home. Had the local police check his apartment and contact friends. At the moment his whereabouts are unknown."

"Ah, that's it. Domingo has to be tied into the shuttle deal somehow. How much do you want to bet he has disappeared?"

"I wouldn't bet against you. In fact, I have called Roy

Borden back from Houston. He is on his way to San Luis Obispo to determine if the man is missing. He remembers Domingo Von Kamp from work they did together for NASA. There will be no fooling him with a double. We will know soon if Domingo has disappeared."

"I bet he has," Steve said confidently. "I don't know why or what his connection with the shuttle is, but I guarantee our young Mr. Von Kamp has disappeared. If he's not missing, I'll admit I'm wrong and come home to work on a new angle."

Confident that they had a suspect, Steve hung up the phone, put it aside, and returned to playing his feeble role.

"Got to work. . . . Can't let myself fall asleep. Can't . . ."

"But you must."

Tanya leaned closer, and he drew her down until their lips met. Hers were hot and moist. It was enough to drive everything else from his mind. She too was lost in the mellow mood and didn't resist while he rolled over and maneuvered until their bodies met along their entire lengths. She wore no bra. That was unlike her, and he could feel her nipples harden as he moved slowly, massaging them gently with his bare chest.

"Oh, Steve," she whispered.

"Tanya." The dialogue was from an early soap opera.

"Does it hurt?" she asked.

"No." He played the brave hero who endured pain for his mission. "You make me forget how much it does hurt," he sighed.

Then she felt the hardening rod in his shorts. Momentarily she pressed her hips forward. Then she rolled and leaped from the bed.

"You bastard," she said. "You're not hurt."

"Not hurt? I'm bruised. I was shot."

"Shot, hell."

"Well, not seriously."

"Not seriously enough to keep you from screwing any broad who happens to be around."

"Hey! I'm damned particular who I screw. Treat your body right and it'll always amuse you. That's my code."

"Well, I don't give one damn about your code." She flung the washcloth at his face. "You're not adding me to your list of conquests by flaunting a few bruises. Get your own bandages. And some sleep. You might meet an easy lay right in the middle of our mission, and we can't have you too tired to participate."

She reached the door and slammed it behind her.

Steve sat up in the bed and tossed the wet cloth aside.

"Damn," he said.

How was he ever going to get to sleep now?

Roy Borden landed the company jet at San Luis Obispo's only airport, hired a car, and drove into the clean, quiet university town north of Los Angeles. With a few blocks of commercial district to serve the locals and the surrounding ranchers, it was a pleasant city where the pace seemed slower.

Guided by a map that came with the rented car, he drove directly past the college and into an area of rolling hills where many of the faculty lived.

He headed to the address he had been given, although, having discussed the matter with Adam, he had no expectation of finding Domingo Von Kamp at home. Instead he had prepared himself with a few simple tools that would get him into the house so quickly the neighbors wouldn't even notice.

He had no idea what he expected to find inside.

But there would be something. A man could rarely leave his home for an extended period without dropping some hint that could put an investigator on the trail. And while Roy was an engineer, not a private eye, he had worked so many special cases for Adam Crown that he had developed a keen sense for tracking. The methodical technical approach ingrained in him served him well.

Carrying his tools in his pocket, he parked the car outside a small Spanish-style house with a high fence around it, checked the address on the mailbox, and got out.

He walked to the front door, rapped twice with the brass knocker, and pushed the doorbell button several times. Then he took his tools and bent toward the lock, anxious to get started.

He was glad for a lead. Time was running out rapidly for those in the shuttle.

The door opened.

"Yes?" A voice said from inside.

Startled, Roy straightened up with a foolish grin on his face.

"I was looking for . . ." He blinked. He wasn't prepared to believe it, but there was no doubt.

It was him. "Well, good morning, Domingo." Roy's words were delivered in a fast staccato as he tried to hide his shock. "Remember me? Roy Borden from Crown General Corporation?"

Domingo Von Kamp said, "Yes, of course. Won't you come in?"

Chapter 12

CORPUS Cristi drove the Mercedes past the high-rise apartment buildings, down streets of humble homes and wretched hovels, beyond the edge of the city, and finally on to the pampas, where the unending plains were a black void at night.

Ten miles out in the pampas, she turned into a grove of trees and stopped at a gate hidden from the road. Outside a guard's tower, a watchman was caught in the headlights wadding a piece of paper. He flung it to the ground and stomped on it, cursing it and blaming himself for ever having bought it.

"A lottery ticket," Cristi said over her shoulder. "The more you abuse it, the better it treats you."

The guard thrust the abused ticket in his pocket and opened

the gate after a cursory inspection of the car's occupants.

"I feel like an interloper," Tanya said as they rolled past a wall of trees, around a curve in the narrow lane, and along a vast lighted lawn edged with flower gardens.

Steve reassured her again. "I told you. Miguel Marcelo insisted you join us tonight. He represents Crown General, after all. He's bound to entertain any visitors from the home office."

"Hmmm." Tanya half agreed.

She was studying the sprawling English-style mansion. They could see only the main house clearly, but there were obviously servant quarters, garages, stables, and other buildings to the rear. The opulence was wisely hidden from the poor Indians and working class mestizos—the half whites, half Indians.

"If he's so rich," she thought aloud, "why does he work for Crown? The Marcelos are one of the Argentine two hundred."

"The what?"

"The top two hundred families of Argentina. Most of the money, ultimately all of the power," Tanya explained. "The men belong to the Jockey Club and the women to the *Sociedad de Beneficencia*. Perón burned the Jockey Club, and Evita put society ladies in jail with prostitutes after they snubbed her as a peasant. But all that has changed back."

"He doesn't work full-time for Crown, does he?"

"No," she began to answer her own question. "He lends his name when Crown has any dealings down here. But what about us? Why are we here when we should be working the shuttle problem?"

Steve said, "I need help in tracking Von Kamp. I can't bully my way around down here like I can some places."

"But the shuttle only has so much time."

The car door was opened by a servant dressed like a Victorian butler. Rich Argentines still lived the life lost by British country gentlemen a generation before.

He greeted them in Spanish and led them to the house. Corpus Cristi remained with the car.

"Ah, Señorita Horton and Señor Crown." Miguel Marcelo welcomed them into a long foyer hung with paintings of bullfighters and generals in heavily braided and medal-bedecked uniforms. "Good heavens, Don Steve, your face! Bruises, and that streak on your cheek. I heard you had been hurt."

"Oh, did you?" From whom, Steve wondered.

"Yes, and I apologize for my countrymen. We are a troubled people. But we will speak of that later. This way, *por favor*."

He led them into a room dominated by a huge fireplace and windows that showed the house had walls two feet thick. The furnishings were elegant rather than ostentatious, but before he could take in the art that adorned the walls, Steve was being introduced along with Tanya.

Señora Marcelo was younger than her husband's fifty-two years, but not by much. She became a gracious, smiling, but nearly silent hostess in the presence of her tall, dark, and regal husband. Her hair was as gray as his, yet his gave him distinction; hers merely added age. They dressed formally, her neck and wrists a storehouse of gold, diamonds, and precious stones imbedded in necklaces and bracelets.

"In honor of our *norteamericano* guests, we dispense with our usual formalities," Marcelo began. "We have starved you already with our late dinner hour—unforgivable thoughtlessness on my part. You shall call me Don Miguel. My wife Doña Estela. My daughter Anjelica. And . . ."

Steve Crown liked the next introduction.

Anjelica was a dark-haired beauty subduing a sensual spirit in a social corset, he was certain. Her dark eyes glistened with interest when she first saw him, then dulled with disappointment when she saw Tanya. She seemed to assume he was attached with leg irons of some kind to his grandfather's able assistant.

He tested the premise, making several remarks that showed there was no romantic attachment between him and Tanya. The girl's eyes revealed interest again.

She might know some things about Argentina that her parents wouldn't, Steve convinced himself. He would have to see her alone—in the interest of the mission, of course.

Miguel Marcelo was introducing the other guest at the intimate dinner party. Conte Ramirez, who had another string of names too, was forty, balding, squint-eyed, and suspicious.

Steve thought he knew why.

"Are you any relation to former president Ramirez?"

"Yes." Don Conte's slightly hunched shoulders pushed back as if he recalled he too was from the former ruling oligarchy.

Another coincidence? Steve asked himself. He spent his first night at the tomb of the late president, then met the son for dinner the second evening. Coincidence? Impossible.

Don Miguel brilliantly read his business associate's mind.

"I learned from Corpus Cristi that you were interested in meeting President Ramirez," the host said openly. "I apologize for her misinterpretation of your request. It was an innocent mistake on her part considering our respect for the dead."

"Corpus Cristi reports to you?" Steve asked coldly.

It didn't disturb Marcelo. "She called me after realizing she had unwittingly exposed you to danger. She was afraid the authorities would hear of your innocent involvement with the Peronistas and revoke your visa. I assured her I would intercede if a problem arose."

Steve deliberately hesitated. What should he think about his two contacts—supposedly strangers until yesterday—conferring about him behind his back?

He decided to let the matter go. "I see," he said.

They finished their drinks and entered a dining room with a table so long that conversation from one end to the other would be impossible if all the chairs were filled.

The Marcelos assumed positions at opposite ends while the others were seated in the center: Steve and Anjelica on one side, Tanya and Conte Ramirez on the other.

The dinner became a feast of beef, soup, and salads. Don Conte steered the conversation to what interested him.

"You wanted to see my father about something," he said. "Perhaps I could help."

"Yes," Marcelo said. "You haven't confided the purpose of your trip to Argentina, Don Steve. If it is influential people you wish to meet . . ."

Steve pondered. How far did he dare go in admitting the truth? The U.S. government still had not made public the threat against the shuttle. So he limited himself to a bit of the truth.

"I don't imagine you're familiar with the names of the astronauts aboard the current space shuttle."

"Carlotta Von Kamp," Anjelica said. "I remember the woman's name."

"My daughter is too modern for her old-fashioned parents," Don Miguel said. "She longs for adventure. But you are correct. I for one am not familiar with any of the names."

Conte Ramirez agreed. "Nor I," he said. He frowned. Anything but a handsome man, his dour expression of puzzlement squeezed his face into a big facsimile of a raisin, wrinkled and dark. "You mention the space shuttle and inquire about my father. I do not see the connection. My father died years ago."

"Yes, but there is a link." Steve smiled at Anjelica. "I referred to Carlotta—as you call her—the astronaut. You see, her father has disappeared."

"His name was Eric Von Kamp," Tanya added.

"I don't believe I ever heard of him," Don Miguel said.

His wife spoke tentatively from the far end of the table.

"A German. He married an Argentine actress."

Steve's hopes rose. "Yes, that's the man."

"They had . . . how would you say it, a *parte de amor*."

"A love nest?" Tanya suggested.

"*Sí*, that is right. Near Iguassú Falls. It was a great scandal during the war. A Nazi here, flaunting his mistress. I was young then." Doña Estela smiled. "The woman, I admired her acting. So beautiful, and the German was handsome in his uniform. I was shocked, too, of course."

"But he did marry her?" Steve said.

"Yes, eventually, like Perón and that woman of his."

Steve continued. "Anyway, that wife died, and he remarried. Carlotta Von Kamp—or Charlotte, as she goes by now—was born of his American wife, also now dead."

"Very complicated," Conte Ramirez said. "I still see no connection with my father."

"With Eric Von Kamp having disappeared—at such a crucial time in his daughter's life—naturally all of us in the government and the space industry are concerned. We would like to find him before his daughter has to be told he is missing."

"That is police work, no?" Miguel Marcelo said.

"Mr. Von Kamp had a ticket to Argentina. So there is a chance he came here. For whatever reason. Tanya and I volunteered to check out that lead for the authorities, since a missing person doesn't justify sending police around the world. I imagine they had notified your police to be on the lookout for him, but for the girl's friends and fellow workers, that is not enough. So Tanya and I came to Buenos Aires to see if we could do something. And, unfortunately, all we know about Von Kamp's life here is that he knew President Ramirez."

"So you tried to see my father?" Conte Ramirez said.

"Yes."

"And he is dead."

"It doesn't leave much for you to go on," Marcelo said. "But I will use my influence with our authorities. If you have a picture and his passport number, we should be able to track him."

"I have his picture," Steve said.

Tanya chimed in. "And I brought his passport number."

"Send both around to my office in the morning."

Conte Ramirez volunteered too. "And I will inquire of my father's friends. Perhaps they know something of Von Kamp."

"Could you track down the marriage license? I believe it was issued in Buenos Aires in 1944. It would give us a lead to any of his first wife's family who might be alive. There's a remote chance that he simply came down to visit them."

"But, of course," Conte Ramirez said. "It will be my pleasure. Anything for the astronauts."

"They will be orbiting over Argentina most of the time now," Anjelica said. "I wish we could see them."

"Perhaps there's a tracking station in the area," Steve suggested. "I could arrange for you to use their telescope."

Tanya Horton cast an accusatory glance in his direction.

It was bull. He hadn't any intention of taking Anjelica Marcelo to a tracking station. He doubted that the girl believed him even as she responded.

"That would be delightful. Could I go, Father?"

"When?" Marcelo asked. If he was suspicious, he didn't let it show. Perhaps he was not as protective of his daughter as wealthy Latins normally were.

"It would have to be tomorrow," Steve told him. "If you and Mr. Ramirez don't come up with a lead on Von Kamp in twenty-four hours, I'll have to put all my time into finding him."

He turned his attention back to Anjelica.

"Tomorrow about noon?" he suggested. "That should give me time to find a station and arrange transportation."

"Wonderful!" Anjelica beamed.

"You can see a space shuttle during the day?" Doña Estela questioned innocently.

Steve was quick to correct himself. "Oh, no, we won't be home before dark. Is that all right, Don Miguel?"

The father frowned. "When I was my daughter's age, there were still *dueñas* for such occasions."

"But this is today, Father."

"Be careful," Miguel Marcelo cautioned. "As you learned last night, Don Steve, Argentina is again in a tenuous position."

"But it isn't the season." Steve quoted Corpus Cristi.

Marcelo laughed. "True. It is not the season for revolt."

A final exchange of glances and the date was finalized. Knowing he would see her again, Steve was certain not to pay undue attention to Anjelica through the rest of the evening.

And the subject didn't come up again until he and Tanya were back at the hotel and walking down the corridor to their rooms.

"You know there's no tracking station in the area," she accused him.

"No!" He pretended to be surprised.

"You just want to spend the day with that girl."

They had reached her door, and she started to unlock it, then changed her mind. He leaned forward, a hand on either side of her. She tipped her head to one side away from him.

"Relax," he teased. "I'm not going to kiss you."

"Damn you!" she said.

"For what? For trying to kiss you or for not trying?"

"You're going to waste a day with her."

"I'd prefer to waste it with you, if I thought you'd pull dowr the wall between us and see what comes through."

She turned and inserted the key in the lock. "No. Four people's lives depend on us. I'm going to spend every moment trying to save them and the space program."

She had started through the door, and he prevented her from closing it on his face.

"Anjelica is taking me to Iguassú Falls tomorrow," he snapped at Tanya. "Where Von Kamp had a house once, remember."

She looked relieved. She didn't want to think the worst of him.

"I'll have Cristi charter a plane for us and arrange a car," he said.

"Overnight accommodations too?"

"Yes."

That she didn't like. "Cristi will put you up in an adobe hut with pigs running in and out. It'll suit you perfectly."

"Don't underestimate her. I saw her slide through gunfire like water through a sieve twice in twenty-four hours."

"She also went through Stanford."

Steve was astounded. "She what?"

"You ought to know your guides better. There was a file on her, you know."

"She told me she was raised by Indians."

"She was. She got scholarships and help from exiled Argentine millionaires living in the States."

"And buys guns for us."

"Yes," Tanya said. "Makes you wonder what else she does for others."

"Don't ask," he said.

"She comes highly recommended."

"By whom?"

Tanya raised her eyes as if the answer were high on the wall. "I don't know. I ought to ask your grandfather that."

"Well, she can make arrangements for me. A separate room for the girl. Her father's going to raise enough hell when she and I stay the night, even if I put her up in a nunnery."

Still Tanya was angry.

"All right," he said. "Join us there. Just don't let Anjelica see you."

"You flake," she said. "I have no intention of following you about on one of your liaisons."

"Bring a gun."

"What?"

"Look. I almost got killed twice last night. That was after I had been in the country for no more than a couple of hours."

"Am I supposed to hold off the irate Argentine father and his shotgun?"

"You know damned well I wouldn't waste a minute on that broad if it weren't part of the mission."

"Ha!" she scoffed.

"Eric Von Kamp had property at Iguassú Falls," he said. "And right now I can't think of one other damned place to start searching for him. Can you?"

"But you don't need the girl for that."

"I need an interpreter. And I need you. With a gun."

"Why?"

"Because someone may try to shoot me in the back."

"You'll carry one too?"

"No."

"Because you'll be naked—in bed with that girl. Damn you, Steve Crown, just when I think there's some hope for us . . ."

She slammed the door, and he pounded on it several times.

"Tanya, listen. Tanya!" Aw, hell, he thought. She was right. He couldn't stay faithful to one woman.

But for Tanya he might try.

Do it. He told himself. With the shuttle's fate in his hands, he shouldn't waste a minute anyway. To hell with women. He needed his sleep.

He swung open the door of his room and fumbled for the light switch.

"*Buenos noches, Don Steve*," Corpus Cristi said from the darkness. "You ready to put out a fire?"

"Aw, shit," he said.

Chapter 13

FROM the space shuttle, Charlotte Von Kamp spoke into the scrambler mike with growing frustration.

"I want to know the truth about my father. What's happened to him? What's he done?"

In Houston, Mission Control director Fred Yarkin breathed in heavily.

"He hasn't done anything except issue the bomb warning."

"He's holding us for ransom? I don't believe that."

"No, no. Nothing like that."

Floating above the seat in front of her, Commander James Carlyle watched her carefully. She was breathing deeply, abnormally so. A woman, he thought. They should never have brought along a woman. She might panic yet.

"Something wrong, Jim?" Alex Bunyan asked.

"No, why?"

"You're breathing hard."

Just like the girl. Carlyle pulled himself around to check the gauges. A soft warning beeper started. Red lights went on.

Jim Carlyle and his pilot leaned forward to check.

On the speaker, the Mission Control director repeated what little he knew about Charlotte's father.

"Since he called about the bomb, we haven't been able to contact him. He's probably at a neighbor's watching your flight."

"You're not telling me the entire truth," Charlotte said.

"All right. We do have reason to believe that he might have gone to Argentina. Possibly against his will. When the FBI went to check his house, they were fired on from inside."

"By my father?" Her pitch was rising sharply.

"No, of course not. The house was burned, two men killed."

"Oh, my God."

"Don't panic. Neither man was your father. And we have the FBI and all state and local police looking for him. We can't mention his name to local authorities, but we have his description out and pictures on the way. And we have the Argentine officials helping us. We'll find him, I promise."

"What about my brother? Have you told him about Dad?"

"Yes. A company engineer who had worked with Domingo—"

"I always call him 'Dom.'"

"Anyway, this gentleman went to see Dom. He told him."

"I want to talk to my brother," Charlotte demanded.

The Mission Control director considered the request briefly, wondered if he should consult someone at a higher level, and then decided against delay.

"All right, Charlotte. But don't worry if we can't get a call through to him right away. He's out of the house a lot."

"He's as worried about my father as I am," she said.

"He's doubly worried, Charlotte. He has you as well as your father to be concerned about."

Commander Carlyle took a mike and interrupted. "Sorry to add coals to the fire, but I'm afraid we have an oxygen leak in tank number one."

"Add tank number two to that," Alex Bunyan said with all the control he could muster.

Arnold Dumas expressed the feelings of the entire crew more aptly. "Aw, no, what next?"

"Confirm that, Jim. Do I read you right? You have oxygen leaks in two tanks."

Carlyle pulled himself closer to the prime gauges while Alex checked redundant instrumentation.

"Confirmed, Control," he said. "Either we've got leaks or there's a crowd here breathing heavy that we don't know about."

"Damn!" The exasperation came from earth loud and clear.

"Anybody mind if I get off and take a subway?" Arnold Dumas said.

"I'm getting the same reading down here, shuttle. Abnormal oxygen loss," Yarkin said. "Hold on while we check the rate."

Charlotte looked up from her private worries. "What do you think caused that—our poking around for the bomb?"

Jim Carlyle shrugged. "We had hatches off. How about it, Alex? Any chance something got inside the tanks?"

"Like a meteor?" Alex furrowed his brow. "Anything's possible. No sound out there. A stone, a piece of scrap from an old satellite—anything could have poked a hole in the tanks, me included."

"Shuttle, this is Mission Control. We have the rate of loss computed. No immediate danger. You have enough aboard to complete your major work schedule."

"Excuse me, Chief," Commander Carlyle said. "You forget we were going for an extended flight."

Yarkin sounded sad as he said, "No, I didn't forget, Jim. The extended schedule is out. In fact, I'm thinking about bringing you down immediately."

"What about the bomb?"

"Probably the same guy who placed the bomb—if there is one—rigged the tanks. Or it could be coincidental failure. We'll be looking into the possibility, but maybe we ought to bring you down now. At the first available landing site."

"How much time have we got left?" Charlotte asked.

Jim Carlyle leaned toward one of the computers.

"I don't need a computer," Alex said. "We sit down in forty-eight hours or this will be the first space hearse in history."

"Just a minute," the voice from earth said. "I'm getting an absolute maximum flight time. Here it is. Your last reentry starts over South America at sixteen hundred hours, day after tomorrow, Pacific Standard Time. Repeat, last reentry starts at precisely sixteen hundred hours, launch time. That's using everything you've got including the oxygen in your space suits. Do you want to return sooner?"

"Oh, my God," Carlyle whispered. For a moment he lost his icy control. The days, actually weeks, that they could stay aloft searching for a way to defuse the bomb had just been cut to hours. It was as if a condemned man had applied for a stay and received an earlier date with the noose instead.

Carlyle looked from face to face. He could take a vote, but he'd be shirking his own duties. It wasn't much of a choice. Gamble on further oxygen loss or gamble on the bomb.

"Okay, Control. We'll stay up as long as possible to see if you can defuse this little firecracker we think we have aboard."

"Roger," Yarkin said. "You're confirmed to begin reentry at sixteen hundred hours, launch time, day after tomorrow. I'll start preparations here."

When he had released the button that activated his mike, Fred Yarkin sank back in his chair. He rested for a moment, then picked up another phone and waited for an answer. His hands were shaking, his body wet with perspiration. Forty-eight hours.

"Mission Control here," he said when he heard a click in the receiver. "Did you monitor my last transmission?"

"Yes, Fred," a voice from Washington answered. "We got it, and we're putting everybody the bureau has left on this new complication. But you know what forty-eight hours means."

"Have you anything new on the bomb?" Fred Yarkin asked.

"Not much," came the response. "But we agree that a timer-controlled detonator would not jibe with Von Kamp's warning to keep the shuttle airborne until the problem can be corrected."

"You think it's an altitude-activated detonator, then?"

"That or ground controlled."

"Radio?"

"Yeah, wouldn't take much. A tiny one-channel receiver on the shuttle."

"Whoever put the bomb aboard would need a transmitter."

"Yes. Again it wouldn't take much. Pray that's the way it works. That gives us a chance to track down whoever intends to send the detonator signal. We'd be fighting someone on the ground, not a device a hundred miles up that nobody can reach."

"Anything on the Argentina angle?" Fred asked hopefully.

His contact in Washington replied, "That's not in my jurisdiction, Fred. State or the CIA must be working on that angle. But everybody here considers it a false lead to divert our resources. What would Argentina have to do with our space shuttle?"

"I don't know."

"What's that time again?"

"Sixteen hundred hours, day after tomorrow. That's the last minute they can start down and still survive."

"Aw, fuck," the voice from security groaned. "And we're getting nowhere."

Yarkin laid the phone aside and stared at the big map of the world at the front of the room. He was watching the curved line showing the shuttle move up over South America. With each orbit it moved slightly farther east.

Well, there was one good thing. The last orbit would put the spacecraft in good position to land at either Edwards Air Force Base in the desert or Vandenberg's own newly extended thirteen-thousand-foot runway.

She would come right up over Argentina, then across the Caribbean and down into California. Or she'd blow before she flew across the Amazon.

A man with a clipboard close to Yarkin finished making notations from several displays and walked on. He checked more telemetry data before heading to the rest room.

When he was certain he was alone, he took the lid off the metal dispenser of paper towels and extracted a miniaturized citizen's band radio. He pressed the transmit button and spoke without waiting for a response.

"Gotta change our date, babe. Pick you up after I get off work day after tomorrow. At four P.M. Sorry, babe, gotta go."

He wiped his fingerprints from the transmitter and returned it to the towel dispenser. He whistled as he returned to the control room.

Chapter 14

STEVE Crown drove the winding road from the Marcelo mansion in a Mercedes convertible that Corpus Cristi had rented for him, the warm wind blowing Anjelica's long black hair while she smiled, looking forward to her day of freedom with the American.

"You don't know how stifling Argentina can be," she said.

"For someone in your social circle?" Steve asked.

"In the United States, women are so free. They don't restrict their lives to family and a few close friends."

He passed the gate and turned toward the city. She didn't know it, but he was heading for the airport and a chartered plane.

"You've been to the States?" he asked.

"I lived there for four years while I went to college."

"That's why your English is so good."

"Yes. When I am with someone like you, I think in English. Today I forget my Spanish."

Feeling guilty, Steve told her, "I couldn't find a tracking station for us to visit."

She smiled. "I didn't think you would."

"But you came anyway?"

"It will be good to be Americanized again, even if it is only for a day. Where *are* we going?"

"Iguassú Falls. I rented a plane."

"It's beautiful there." It was the only approval she gave.

"I want to look in on the property owned by Eric Von Kamp."

"You can't give up your search for a day?"

"Not completely. Do you think you could find it?"

She said, "Of course. Everyone knows where it is. But no one goes near it."

"Oh? Why?"

"People die there," she said.

"How?"

"Accidents. Three people died once from gas. Others burned to death."

"You make it sound cursed."

She nodded. "To the superstitious, yes. They say Von Kamp didn't really have it built, that it was built by Perón for his mistress, Maria Gallardo. Recently, people say they have proof Perón actually married her, not Von Kamp, and that is why Perón couldn't marry Evita until 1945—until Maria died in Germany. Others say Von Kamp built the house. That it was to be Hitler's vacation home after they won the war."

"Or his hiding place if he lost?"

She laughed. "No, the place has been searched many times, by the Israelis mainly, but no Nazis are there. Most of the time no one is there. The guards collect their pay for nothing. No one goes near the awful place."

"Are you afraid of it?"

"No. I might be afraid to go alone. Argentine men don't go there either, alone or in groups."

"Good, then I'll enjoy myself more, feeling like I'm your protector."

Steve slowed the car as they approached the shacks along the edge of the city. Normally at midday the people would be sleeping or resting somewhere cool, but today they were gathered in the street.

At the head of every small group, a man was either haranguing the people about Perón or leading them in a chant.

"Perón rises again," they were saying in Spanish. "It is the resurrection."

"What's all this about?" Steve asked.

People shook their fists at him and the expensive car. They spit on the potholed pavement as close to the wheels as they could.

"My mother would say the people are getting *atrevido*—impertinent again. My father would say they are poor because they are stupid."

"And you—what would you say?"

"That there will be another revolution. The oligarchy ruled for generations, then we got Perón. He delivered so much to the workers, made such a saint of his wife, that the country drowned in inflation. So the army tried again, several times. Now the army wants to turn the government over to the civilians, but they outlawed the Peronistas as too radical, even though they have no leader. No Perón."

"So they want to resurrect him."

"Probably Evita," she said. "Peronistas stole her coffin, you know. They will show her corpse and claim she has risen or some such nonsense, hoping the people will follow."

"Will they?"

"Follow a corpse? No. Not this time. The army will recapture the coffin, and the revolution will falter."

"Too bad he wasn't a king. He could have left Argentina an heir to his throne."

"Yes."

They reached the airport, where a massive crowd had gathered. Police were moving into position to disperse them.

"More blood," Anjelica said sadly.

As he parked the car, Steve listened to a wild-faced young man screaming at his followers.

He was saying nothing different except for a few words that he repeated over and over.

"Mañana. Mañana. La resurrección. Ocho y treinta."

"Do I understand him correctly?" Steve asked as they walked toward the four-place aircraft he had rented. "Is he setting a time for this resurrection."

"Yes, eight-thirty tomorrow night. On the main street of the city. So soon. I wouldn't have believed it. There will be fighting surely. So brazen to name a time and a place. It shows the ignorance of the Peronistas. They expect to stand off an army with a coffin."

"They'll need more than that."

"Someone they can follow, not a body."

Steve looked back once more at the crowd. The world was filled with people so unlike himself. While he worked to save four astronauts attempting to push on to new frontiers, these people were looking to a corpse to lead them.

But his own people were no more clever. One of them—probably far more than one—wanted to destroy the space shuttle.

Why?

If he knew that, he might know who had planted the bomb. Knowing that, he could stop them. But all he could do now was go on a wild chase after one man.

From the air the Iguassú Falls were one of the most overwhelming sights he had seen in a lifetime of traveling.

Dipping the small aircraft to within several hundred feet of the spectacular sight, he measured it against other falls he had seen. Near the point where several rivers joined, there were widespread cataracts in the virgin forests bright with orchids and serpentine creepers draped from the branches of the trees.

Thirty streams and rivers coursed through the plateau, then met and flowed around hundreds of wooded islets to create 275 separate falls, each taller than Niagara—wider, too, by half. And above them hovered a perpetual mist created by the water splashing on the basalt rock.

"Look," Anjelica said, pointing to the rainbow painted by the afternoon sun.

That sight too was spectacular, and Steve flew low across the face of the falls, turning back before he crossed into Brazilian air space. His permit to fly had been endorsed only by the Argentines.

The river below the falls was dotted with dozens of small islands, many accessible by board walkways. He circled over them before landing at the airport near the Hotel Catarata. From there, they picked up a rental car and drove back along the river road, leaving it just short of Port Iguassú. They turned up an unmarked, single-car lane that Anjelica recognized.

It wove through a thick forest, impenetrable on foot because of the undergrowth. But as they rose over a ridge, Steve caught sight of an aging mansion rising from a shaved-off hill. He could see only the top, but there was a widow's watch and dormer windows. The facing was stucco, painted a now faded and peeling white. The trim was a dull gray, with some of the lower wooden strips torn off by storms or perhaps by the poor gathering firewood.

It was the kind of place that invited stories of the rich and the cruel, the powerful and the dead.

But why did it sit there vacant? he wondered.

Everything about Eric Von Kamp was strange. A single call to save his daughter. His disappearance. His indirect connection to Perón.

The man's past was a snarl of unanswered questions. But did he have time to look back? Steve asked himself. He was having enough difficulty with the present and the future. The space shuttle crew couldn't wait forever. Yet he didn't know where else to look.

"That's it?" he asked.

"Yes."

"It looks . . ." How did it look? Eerie? Yes. Like a recluse hiding deep in a closet of trees.

"Haunted," she said for him.

"Yes."

They passed through a gateway in a towering stone wall topped with steel spikes, but with the gate itself torn from its hinges and left lying in the weeds.

"I suppose it's been looted long ago," Steve said aloud.

"No. For a long time it was guarded by men with guns and vicious dogs. Then by several old men. Scavengers who attempted to make off with the furnishings came to bad ends. Today everybody stays away." She had sudden second thoughts. "We should too."

Steve glanced away from the road to see her fear, and in his peripheral vision caught sight of another car rushing toward them.

Instinctively he twisted the Volkswagen's wheel and drove down into the ditch as the oncoming Toyota kicked his rear bumper and dashed on through the exit.

"That bastard!" Steve never slowed down. He cramped the wheel and came up out of the ditch in a tight U-turn. He could see two men in the car, but he recognized neither of them. One might have been Von Kamp.

His heart pounded with excitement. He might be getting close to the break he needed.

Gambling that his quarry was in the other car, he raced after it, Anjelica hanging on, crying for him to slow down.

At the main road the Toyota careened into a skidding turn back toward the airport and the Hotel Catarata. As they passed the airport, the lead car made a feint at turning south, then took the hard left toward the hotel.

Here the two lanes were crowded with tourist buses, jeeps, and private cars. The driver of the Toyota jammed his brakes and went into a skid. When the Toyota stopped, the men jumped out and sprinted toward the edge of the cliff that overlooked the falls. Their car effectively blocked the road, and Steve had to jump a curb before getting the Volkswagen stopped.

It was only then that he realized Anjelica was screaming.

She was yelling in Spanish. He couldn't translate fast enough, but obviously she couldn't imagine what had turned him into a reckless fool.

"Gotta get those men!" he shouted at her. "Stay here."

"No. I'm going with you."

He doubted if she could keep up, and he plunged between giant rock formations, following a serpentine path that wound down toward the river's edge. The walk was wet and slick. A slip could send him plunging down a cliff. The roar of the falls became more deep-throated and intense, ominous in the power the sound represented.

A few yards along the rock path he came upon the paved walk from the hotel. It was crowded with people headed in both directions.

In his rush he knocked elbows, forced himself ahead of others, and ignored the multilingual cursing of those he handled roughly. There were whites and Orientals. Blacks and Arabs in robes. Schoolchildren in groups.

For all of them, their pleasant sightseeing tour had suddenly been transformed into frightening chaos. The men ahead of Steve had already bulled their way through, leaving a few minor casualties along the way. A child was crying. An old woman had been knocked to the concrete. A man had slipped beneath the guardrail and had nearly plunged over the precipice into the surging river.

A few people pressed against rocks or stepped into the thick vegetation to make way for Steve.

Anjelica was following him still, but, unable or unwilling to force her way, she was rapidly falling behind him.

Steve didn't wait for her. The chase had renewed his confidence. He was certain the two men had been waiting for him at the deserted mansion, and he was equally certain they were luring him into some sort of trap. He doubted they were trying to lose themselves in the crowd, although he could barely keep them in sight.

As for whatever trap they had in mind, he had to chance it. He couldn't believe they weren't somehow involved in his mission. Why else would they run from him?

Because they had been found looting the closed mansion that Von Kamp had purchased years before? Possibly. But thieves would try to escape, not plunge into a crowded dead end.

Convinced, he raced through hot humid air that teemed with

butterflies and mosquitoes. Finally the paved path to the river bank ended, and the men ahead paused.

They were reconsidering.

And for a moment Steve thought he had them trapped. There was nothing but the foaming and writhing waters of the river behind them.

"Hold it there," he called.

Together they turned and plunged a few more feet upstream, then darted out on a narrow plank walkway leading toward a small island. As they ran past tourists, they generated havoc. A child slipped and almost dropped into the cascades, her father's fingers tightening around her tiny wrist at the last second.

The planking creaked and tilted.

Steve hesitated, weighing the consequences of the chase. Innocent people might get hurt or killed.

The men might be armed and start shooting into the crowd.

But they were his only lead in the race to save the space shuttle. And who knew the consequences of failure? Anyone willing and capable of such a complex and fiendish act as rigging a bomb on a spacecraft could have plans with national or international consequences.

He gambled his life; others would have to gamble theirs, too.

With renewed determination, he pounded out onto the plank. The men he pursued had disappeared briefly, but he heard the cracking of twigs and the brush of leaves moving across the island to his left.

He came out of the woods closer to the falls.

The men were just ahead of him on another walkway to rocks surrounded with boiling water. They were alone this time. No tourists had taken the same route. Steve saw why. The plank walk they had taken was old. A newer and safer series of short bridges had been built; those led to the right and carried the bulk of the sightseers.

Only the most adventuresome still used the old path with its steel-cable handhold on only one side.

Steve sprinted onto the plank just as the two men left it and circled the rocky islet. Steve went up and over. When he reached the perch he looked down on exactly what he expected—both men flattened against the rock, waiting for him.

Each held a gun.

Christ! He hadn't counted on that. He hadn't wanted Anjelica to catch him wearing a weapon. Instead he had asked Tanya to follow him to the falls, but he doubted if she had.

His action was decided for him. One of the men, hearing or seeing something that caught his attention, looked up. Straight into Steve's eyes.

The rock was ten or eleven feet tall, but Steve lacked choices. The gun was swinging toward him.

He leaped, arms spread like a falcon going for the kill. He had to depend on the men's bodies to cushion his fall.

Each arm caught one of the gunmen, and all three went tumbling off the narrow path around the rock and into the water. A gun fired. Another slipped from its owner's hand. Even as he reached for it, Steve knocked it farther into the roaring river.

The three tried to fight while the current tugged them farther into the rapids. But standing was impossible only a yard from the rock island shore, and survival became everything.

The taller and leaner of the two pursued men broke loose from the water first. He also had the gun, but he ran for the next dilapidated bridge, reaching another island. This one, so close to the torrents of water plunging over the falls, was clouded in mist.

Steve's second target also beat him out of the water, but he slipped on the planking. Steve caught up with him in the middle, slamming him against the cable and nearly upsetting both of them.

They were so close to the falls now that they were in a pelting rain that blurred their vision and made every handhold slippery. It was difficult to stand.

"*Hable*, you bastard." Steve held the stocky man by the throat, pushing him ever closer to a plunge over the cable. "What are you running from? Where's Von Kamp?"

"*No hablo ingles, señor*," the man cried.

"Like hell you don't!"

"*Es verdad. No hablo ingles.*" The man was perspiring from fear and exertion.

"Tell me or you go over the side. Where's Von Kamp?"

"I don't know. I . . ." The man's English was broken but intelligible.

A bullet thumped through the planking, and Steve whirled his prisoner around, pushing him ahead as a shield.

He hadn't counted on the lack of loyalty between the two men. The one on the next islet fired again, deliberately putting a bullet into his cohort's chest.

The wounded man slumped, his limp weight too much to hold. He slipped loose from Steve's grip and went tumbling off the plank and into the river.

He was on his back, his arms thrashing, his mouth open in an inaudible scream. The wound poured a red streak into the foam. He was washed away, and the man on the island fired again.

The bullet missed. The next one or the next wouldn't.

Steve leaped back as if he had been hit and deliberately let himself roll into the water on the side toward the falls. Frantically he tried to get his feet down, but the force of the water pushed them from under him.

As he was being swept back under the plank, he saw his last chance—a support cable that ran from the bottom of the plank to a concrete footing on the island. He reached up, bending his fingers into a hook. Splashing with his arm and feet, he had one pass at the cable. He had to get his hook on the cable the first time. There'd be no second chance. With the water foaming around him, he couldn't see whether he was going to make it or not.

If he missed, he would be beaten to death against the rocks.

The slender man with the gun approached the bridge cautiously. He had no regrets about killing his friend. They weren't really friends, he told himself. They were soldiers in a revolution. One did what one had to do in a war.

He peered into the water, trying to make certain the *norteamericano* had not hung up on a submerged rock a few yards down from where he had fallen.

Good shooting, he told himself. Two hits out of three and under adverse conditions. Even on the bridge, he was in the equivalent of a downpour. In a minute, though, he could throw away the gun and return to the car. Being drenched, he was bound to attract attention. Nobody used the old catwalks any longer, except a few daring children, and they wore rain gear.

If anyone noticed he was alone, the police could easily question him about the chase. He could lie his way out of that, but he could never explain a gun.

Another moment was all he needed.

Kneeling on the wet boards, he leaned over the side, trying to see beneath. He bent farther, holding on with one hand, using the other to keep the gun in front of him, ready to shoot.

He saw Steve Crown's eyes. Nothing more.

Before he could get his muscles into motion, he felt a hand fold around his neck and pull downward.

"No!" he screamed once.

Then his torso toppled over the edge of the walk, thrusting his center of gravity far out over the water, dragging his hips and legs up and over.

He entered the water on his back.

Steve tried to hold him, but the falling body was torn from his grip. He grabbed a piece of cloth and held on; it was slippery wet, and the man's thrashing was his own undoing. The shirt slid through Steve's fingers, and the body went tumbling down the river between the islands.

Pulling himself along the cable until he could touch solid rock with his feet, Steve hauled himself to safety and ran to the far side of the exposed rock.

He could see neither of the men he had pursued in the river.

Then Anjelica was there, throwing herself into his arms, ignoring what his wet clothes were doing to hers, and thanking God for his safety.

"What happened? Who were those men?" She threw questions at him in Spanish and English and combinations of the two.

"*Nada*," he told her repeatedly, at the same time urging her back along the catwalks.

"Tell me," she insisted.

Strangers were staring at his wet clothes, no doubt many of

them remembering he had been one of three men who had run out over the river.

He had to change the questioning mood of the crowd before someone brought in the police.

"A game," he called to the crowd with a smile. "My friends played a prank on me, but they got away."

It didn't matter too much what he said. Few in the crowd could understand English, but his smile was reassuring.

"I thought they were two men who tried to kill me the other night at the cemetery," he lied to Anjelica.

"Were they?"

"I don't know. I lost them when I slipped and fell."

"You're lucky you didn't drown."

"Yeah."

He put his arm around her shoulder and smiled, joking about what a fool he had made of himself. He had her laughing and embarrassed at the public intimacy of his arm, but he could tell she was warming to his wet touch.

Smiling, he was less important to the crowd.

The people began to forget. He was just a foolish foreigner who had fallen into the river.

But laughing and joking weren't easy.

Two more men were dead. Any information they could have given him had drowned with them.

And he partly blamed Tanya Horton. Why hadn't she taken him up on his request and followed him to the tourist attraction? Roy Borden would have. He always was there when you needed him.

Then he thought he saw Tanya in the crowd. She was at the top looking down at him. She turned away and disappeared before he could be sure.

"What do we do now?" Anjelica was asking. "I suppose we could buy dry clothes for you at the hotel."

"I'll dry quickly in this heat," he told her. "I want to go back to Von Kamp's place."

They had reached the top of the hill. Their Volkswagen was still parked up on the curb, but the Toyota Steve had chased had been pushed off the road.

A uniformed officer came rushing over, spewing questions in Spanish.

"Tell him I apologize but I don't speak Spanish," Steve told Anjelica.

She talked for several minutes with the officer before she turned back to Steve.

"He wants to know why we were chasing the Toyota."

Steve pretended innocence, hoping Anjelica would go along with him rather than get involved. "Tell him the crazy driver of the Toyota sped past us and nearly caused a serious accident. I got angry and chased them. The damned fool stopped so fast it was all I could do to avoid hitting him."

She hesitated.

What she finally said, he wasn't certain.

"I told them you chased them down the path, but lost them on one of the islands."

"Yeah, good. That's true. Tell him they're still down there for all I know."

Another brief exchange of words passed between her and the officer before she spoke in English again. "He wants to know, do you intend to file charges? He will go after them if you do."

And maybe find two corpses floating in the river, one with a bullet hole in his chest.

He could spend weeks trying to explain that.

Having pretended to consider the idea, he let himself appear relieved. "No, I guess not. Maybe just a couple of crazy kids. Forget it."

The officer finally tipped his hat, and Steve opened the door for Anjelica. On his side, a piece of paper fell to the ground when he started to get in. He picked it up and read.

He was puzzled.

Written on a Buenos Aires travel agency letterhead, it was an itinerary for a Mr. and Mrs. Carlyle on a flight from someplace abbreviated "EAR." to another airport designated "VAN."

Something left behind by the last user of the rented car, he thought until he saw the travel agent's initials at the bottom.

"T.H."

Tanya Horton?

He read the itinerary again. The departure time struck him. It was the time Shuttle Charlotte had lifted off from earth. . . . Ah, he thought. EAR. Earth. And VAN., Vandenberg Air Force Base.

Tanya had put it in his car door, he figured. So she was here somewhere. Too bad she hadn't been on the islands when he needed her.

"What is that?" Anjelica asked.

"I don't know."

But he was twisting his mind around trying to figure what Tanya had hoped to tell him with a phony itinerary.

The arrival time. And date.

Tomorrow evening at 9 P.M., Buenos Aires time.

The shuttle?

Was that it? The touchdown time for the shuttle. No, probably the moment it started to come down out of orbit. But tomorrow! He thought he had days yet, more than a week.

Why would they come back early? Damn it, what could be accomplished with so little time? He fought off panic.

"It looks important, the way you frown," Anjelica said.

He crumbled the paper and dropped it on the ground with the rest of the litter.

"No, just something someone left in the car."

"Probably the person who rented it yesterday."

"Yeah."

He squeezed his tall body into the cramped car.

"If we return to that place, that house," Anjelica was saying, "will we get back to Buenos Aires tonight?"

He checked his watch. "Fly at night? Might be dangerous," he said. "I suppose your family would kill me if we spent the night at a hotel." He didn't know yet whether he was going to rush back or not, but he was protecting his option to stay if the abandoned house proved interesting.

"Yes," she said.

"What?" His train of thought was still running down the Von Kamp track.

"My father will kill you if we stay. But I will call home. He won't be there yet. I'll leave a message, promising him we will behave." She smiled. "We will, won't we?" It was the type of question he bet she had learned in the States.

"No," he said.

She cocked her head, "Oh, then perhaps we should go home. We—"

"—hardly know each other." He said for her. "Make your call from the hotel. We'll worry about how we behave when we know each other better. And hurry. It'll be dark when we get to the old house as it is."

Unexpectedly she leaned across the seat and kissed him before running to the hotel.

Definitely American educated.

When she was gone, he looked around, searching for Tanya. The crowd was thinning, yet there was no sign of her.

Having given up on that, he tried to make himself comfortable. There had been room enough before. Now it seemed the car had shrunk or he was bloated with river water.

Searching for the seat adjustment lever, he found it with his hand and pushed back.

That was better.

Then he felt the other metal piece beneath the seat.

He ran his fingers along it cautiously, checking for a bomb. It was a possibility to be remembered.

Finally he knew what it was. A gift from Tanya. She had put it there and moved the seat forward so he would put his hand down and find her little present.

Checking around him first, he took the small snub-nosed revolver from beneath the seat and put it behind his belt, covering it with his shirt.

He felt better. Not so much on account of the gun. But it was good, knowing Tanya was in the area.

He was getting close to something important, important enough for two men to trade their lives for.

But they'd been fanatics. Men who valued their lives less than a cause were as dangerous as mad dogs.

There would be more of them, at the house or in Buenos Aires. Everywhere he went, they would be there.

Waiting. To kill him.

Chapter 15

THE Volkswagen reached the break in the mansion wall while the yellow rays of the setting sun were stabbing through spaces among the upper leaves of the tallest trees. The car slowed, rolling between dry fountains that poked above elbow-high weeds.

Before making the last turn, Steve Crown stopped and climbed out. He held his right arm across the front of his shirt at belt level as casually as a man could when he was poised to draw a gun.

"Wait in the car," he told Anjelica.

"You are not going to leave me here alone, are you?"

He didn't blame her. He was nervous even with the pistol. The threat he felt was more cerebral than physical. There was nothing visible, no figure ready to pounce on him. But he could see more of the mansion from here than he had on their first aborted approach, and even discounting the dead-flesh-gray of twilight's end, the house was awesome. It loomed above him, waiting to engulf him if he dared approach too closely.

The threat, he realized, was created by the architect's design. The house had a central peak only slightly taller than the peaks on the wings to either side.

"The German coat of arms," he said aloud.

He had seen it on postage stamps: a warrior design that had been introduced to the Huns by the Roman troops back in ancient times. The house assumed the design when the failing light smothered detail in grayish darkness.

The bird-of-prey design had struck fear into less warlike peoples for centuries, and now it gave Steve Crown a moment's hesitation. He was about to tread on a foreign, sinister soil. He had no idea what the house might conceal.

"Steve." Anjelica was beginning to get out of the car.

"Stay there," he insisted. "I'm just going a few yards up the drive."

Ten more paces and the designer's genius exposed itself. It was no longer just a mansion. To the imaginative viewer, the house was a fierce, belligerent eagle with wings spread, ready to wrap them with bone-crushing force around its approaching prey.

Steve needed to go no farther alone. He could not see a car or a guard in front of the house, nor any recently used driveways leading around to the rear of the main structure. There were no lights showing from inside.

Chances are, it's deserted, he told himself. The two men who had died at the falls were probably the only assassins lying in wait, but he intended to approach with caution.

Returning to the car, he fended off Anjelica's questions and drove closer until he could back the Volkswagen behind a stand of trees, concealing it with the front pointed out. He might want to exit as quickly as his two dead pursuers.

"We walk from here," he told Anjelica.

"Why? Wouldn't it be safer to have the car with us?"

He let her question go.

Toting her big handbag, she ran to keep up. Nearer the house, she took his hand. He stepped to the other side of her, freeing his right hand to grab his gun if necessary.

"You're afraid too," she said, surprised.

"Might be guards. Maybe guard dogs. Do you want to wait in the car? I'll leave you the keys."

"No, I want to see too." She pressed closer to him.

"All the windows are grated," he remarked when he noticed the decorative wrought-iron grillwork that was so popular in Latin countries.

Anjelica said, "They're boarded, too."

She was right. The windows, some of them with broken glass, were boarded from the inside.

"How can we get in?" she asked.

Steve stepped to the door and rapped hard with the dark, tarnished knocker designed in the shape of a swastika. There was no answer; he expected none. He tried the door. It was locked, and the poor light made it difficult for him to work, but he started cutting at the rotting wood around the bolt recess, using his penknife.

"We shouldn't be doing this," Anjelica said.

"Want to go home?"

She giggled. "No."

The door finally swung open with a grating sound like sand between two moving metal gears. He flattened his back against the wall the way police did when they entered a room where a suspect might be hiding.

"Steve!" His caution had frightened her.

He would have preferred to enter with his gun in his palm, but he left it concealed, keeping his fingers poked slightly through the overlapping front of his shirt for a quick draw.

With two fast steps he was inside and to the left of what little light came in from outside.

"Stay there for a moment," he told Anjelica.

"No." She stepped squarely into the center of the doorway. "I won't be afraid of any empty house."

She moved ahead of Steve into a large marble-floored foyer devoid of furniture and decoration except for fading murals on the walls. The light from the door allowed only an overall impression. The murals were the work of South American artists. He could tell by the bold, larger, and more angular than life portrayals of the human form. And yet they were Aryan in interpretation: all whites, including more blondes than were seen in Argentina. All the figures were those of workmen, farmers, pregnant women, and soldiers engaged in a laborer's war against some undefined enemy.

The soldiers wore German and Argentine uniforms. The similarity of the helmet shape linked the two armies. The Argentines of the 1930s and '40s had been trained by Germans.

At the end of the hall was a wide staircase with rotting carpeting and mahogany balustrades leading to an upstairs balcony and hallway. A dirt-caked window at the top of the stairs let in what little light entered the upper hall, until Anjelica tried a wall switch.

A single bulb in a massive crystal chandelier came on above them, changing the gray to contrasting dark sinister shadows and bright shafts of light.

"Good God," Steve said. "Lights?"

"For the guards," Anjelica suggested.

He doubted it and quickly confirmed his hunch.

The house had not gone unused for years. The dust on the foyer floor was scuffed with shoe marks and littered with papers. Most were sacks, newspapers, or brown butcher paper that had been used to wrap lunches. There were hollow gourds with staffs left in them. They'd obviously been used for maté tea, the Argentine national drink. There were empty beer bottles, many broken, and milk cartons. Black banana peels. The rinds of oranges and the cores of apples.

There were amateurishly printed newspapers and a few stacks of political fliers.

"Peronistas," Anjelica said.

No longer any doubt, Steve thought. Here was the final direct link between Eric Von Kamp and the followers of the dead Argentine dictator. The house had obviously been used for a headquarters.

One more link to go. The tie-in to the space shuttle.

Given that, Steve would no longer have any doubts that he

was on the right track. But how he would use the track to save the astronauts was a tougher problem.

Still probing, he tried one of the three sets of double doors that led off the foyer.

Locked.

"Turn off the light," he told Anjelica.

"Must we?"

He knew how she felt. The dark held any grotesque horror the mind cared to create.

She did as she had been told before he tried another door.

The handle, rough from tarnish, turned in his hand. It opened on creaking hinges.

"I don't think we should be here," Anjelica was saying. "Probably the government has taken over the property."

Steve moved into a room. He could see virtually nothing.

"Do you have a match?" he asked the girl. He would have preferred that to a bright bulb.

"No. I don't smoke."

He tried another light switch on the wall. One bulb came on in a lamp sitting in front of a desk.

"The electricity couldn't have been on since Von Kamp built the place," he said.

He walked over to the light. It was in a stand-up lamp set to throw some light on the desk and the rest on the four chairs that had been pulled up around it. Moving the lamp, he checked the chair seats.

Someone's trousers or skirt had dusted the bottom of each chair.

Probably Eric Von Kamp had come here recently, Steve decided. Regardless of how or why he had ordered the place built and furnished during the long-ago war, he might have retained legal title. It would be quite natural, then, for him to come here while he was in Argentina.

Steve felt the rush of excitement. He was getting closer to his quarry. He had Von Kamp's scent. How much of a lead the fox had was another matter.

There was a second important question too: Did the former Nazi know the Peronists were using his house? Those who had favored the Fascists during World War II included Perón, and Perón remained a living corpse in the country's politics. It could have been some of his diehard followers who had kept vandals from the house through the years.

But why?

For a Hitler who never came? For a few of the Führer's henchmen who had escaped the Allied war trials?

Or . . . another idea appealed to Steve. The Peronists might have maintained the place as a sanctuary for their own nefarious dreams and lusts.

Those men in the Toyota—they were Peronists.

Did that make Von Kamp sympathetic to their cause? Possible. But why?

And the house itself. It would have been checked in the early years by all the stalkers of missing Nazi butchers. So the workers dreaming of Perón's resurrection must have used the house only recently.

There was so little touched. Oil paintings of Adolf Hitler in a jaw-clenched pose and Juan Perón in his elaborately decorated, comic-opera uniform adorned opposite walls. Benito Mussolini was relegated to a wall next to the door. There were pictures of Evita Perón, a hint of a halo around her head, and photographs of SS officers herding slave laborers—possibly Jews—into railroad boxcars.

A few of the prisoners' faces were clear, and their eyes stared at Steve, their fear frozen in time. His mind forced him to speculate on their fate following the snapping of the picture.

This—all the brutality the photograph represented—was what Juan Perón had approved with his support for Hitler. Now people—some desperate, some ignorant, some as vicious as Hitler himself—wanted to recreate those bestial days of tyranny.

As he moved the lamp about to the extent of its cord, Steve could see the overstuffed furniture was threadbare from age, not use. The thin layer of dust on the floor was missing wherever furniture sat.

The sealed windows explained the meager film of dust. The scarcity of spiderwebs confounded him at first. Then he realized that their absence confirmed his theory. With no food in the house, there would be few if any bugs for spiders to feed on. So the garbage in the foyer was recent.

Steve checked the working light bulb and several of those that remained dark. Pulling one out and shaking it, he could tell the filament had been broken.

Then he saw the telephone on the desk.

It was the old stand-up type. He picked it up and got a ring that would summon an operator the way phones had worked before the advent of dials.

He handed it to Anjelica. She listened, then hung up.

"Only the very rich can get phones installed these days," she said. "One has to pay the workers and the officials extra."

"Or be a Peronist party leader," he said idly.

"True," she agreed.

He checked more of the room. It was a typical study except for the tattered Nazi flag hanging above the fireplace. He touched the coals. Cold but recently burned, he guessed after smelling his fingers.

Otherwise the room appeared unused.

Eerie, he thought.

A house closed for more than thirty years, used only recently for something.

"Let's look over the rest of the place," he said.

"Why don't you just call out to him?" she asked.

She meant Von Kamp, of course.

"He might hear you if he is in the house," she said.

True.

"Eric!" Steve shouted after he had switched off the light and returned to the entry. The door was still open, providing outside air to freshen the moist, moldy smell of the study. "Von Kamp. Show yourself. I'm a friend."

He started up the staircase, feeling his way with his feet.

"Wait," Anjelica called before she joined him. This time she hooked her hand around his left elbow. Her touch was distracting, and he would have preferred to have the arm free for emergencies.

He squeezed her hand affectionately against his side.

"Fun, isn't it?" he said. "Like visiting a haunted house."

"We say *embrujado*," she said.

They reached a second-floor balcony that extended around three sides, looking down on the floor of the foyer.

Steve felt their way along the walls, opening doors until he found one that was already ajar.

When Anjelica started to speak, he silenced her with a hand to her lips.

He leaned close until his lips were at her ear. "Stay here just one second."

His caution was not for her. He just didn't want to go in the room without the gun in his hand. Even in the dark he couldn't do that if she were hanging on his arm.

He went in quickly, closing the door partially behind himself and swinging the gun muzzle in search of a target. Feeling a wall switch, he knelt and tried it with his left hand. Any instinct shooter would fire at the switch while the sudden light momentarily blinded hunter and quarry alike.

Two lamps came on.

He was in a richly furnished bedroom.

"Can I come in now?" Anjelica asked.

Before he could make the search he would have liked, he stepped to the big bed and slid the gun between the box springs and the mattress.

"Yeah, come on in. Shut the door, though."

She came in curiously.

"It's been used recently," she observed.

She was right. There was no bedding except for two new sheets and one pillow with a fresh cover. The boards had been removed from the windows, and two were open, letting in warm doses of fresh air riding on gentle breezes.

A suitcase lay open on the floor next to the dresser. Steve went over to it and began poking around in the clothes. The first interesting thing he found was a passport. Eric Von Kamp's. Steve pocketed the document. The man he sought wouldn't go far without it.

There were traveler's checks, too. The suitcase had not been unpacked except for a few toilet articles that had been taken into the adjoining bathroom. A cheap metal pitcher of water suggested that the supply to the house had not been turned on.

But the room had definitely been used overnight recently.

There were even several boxes of crackers and cheese sitting out on a dresser.

A chest caught Steve's attention, and he started opening drawers. They were entirely empty. Yet on top sat several photographs. One was of Adolf Hitler. The other was of a woman, an attractive, theatrical-looking woman in her twenties.

She was also in a third photograph that was not in a frame. The large black and white print lay on its back as if it had been tossed there haphazardly. In it the woman stood alongside a youthful Juan Perón. It was not faded or coated with dust and grime accumulated through time like the other two pictures.

"That's her," Anjelica said. "Maria Gallardo. Eric Von Kamp's first wife. Or Perón's wife, if you believe the stories. I recall seeing her picture in old magazines. She was a famous actress from a good family. She must have fallen deeply in love with Von Kamp to leave Argentina for a Germany at war."

"Yeah," Steve agreed.

He had picked up the photograph as though he were touching a snake. Was it poisonous or harmless?

"Perón and the actress," Anjelica said excitedly.

She took the picture.

"This is evidence that Perón was married to her when Evita snared him. The only evidence I've ever seen."

"You're up on this Perón matter, aren't you?"

"Everyone is. In Argentina. Evita and Perón. Our country's greatest love story regardless of one's politics."

Steve took the picture and turned it over. The name of the photographer and a date were printed on the back. A date during World War II. Somehow the lives of the astronauts depended on events that had occurred decades ago and events taking place right now in Argentina. Could he make the connection in a little more than twenty-four hours?

He had to, he told himself. No one else was working on the same angle. There were only himself and Counter Force.

Something bothered Steve about the photo. He couldn't figure what, but he didn't want it to be real. It was too pat, like planted evidence. Was there something wrong in it that he didn't see?

The date? No. Many photographers stamped and dated their work; this printing, however, looked too fresh.

Although the figures filled most of the print, there was enough background to see they were standing in a bedroom; at least, there was a bedspread behind Perón.

"She seems small beside him," Steve observed. "Was she short?"

Anjelica replied, "The pictures I have seen were studio shots. They might have deliberately made her look taller."

"True."

Steve took the photograph over to the light. If he'd had a magnifying glass he would have used that.

"Lucky Strikes," he said, referring to a pack of cigarettes he could barely make out on a table behind the figure of Perón. "I remember old war movies on late-night television. The Germans of World War II were reduced to smoking ersatz cigarettes. American brands were always real treats for the Nazis in the films. But the pack doesn't look quite like the ones I remember seeing," he said. "I wonder if they made a cigarillo back in those days."

"I wouldn't know that either," Anjelica said. Then she pointed to a calendar behind the actress in the picture. "*Diez y nueve, cuarenta y cuatro*," she read.

"Nineteen forty-four. Must have been taken just shortly before she married Von Kamp."

"Is it important?" she said.

"Curious is all," he muttered thoughtfully. "If she and Von Kamp were so much in love, what's a picture of her and Perón doing here?"

He put the photograph back while she asked about the crackers and cheese on top of the chest.

"Do I dare?" she asked.

"Might as well." He joined her in sharing the food. A full bottle of Argentine wine was also on the dresser, and he worked the cork free before finding two glasses in the bathroom. Both had been used recently and not rinsed out. The best he could do was wipe them with a clean towel from the short stack he found in the room. When he returned to the bedroom, he poured wine for both of them and held up his glass in a toast.

"To Eric Von Kamp, our host."

She drank and then asked, "Shouldn't we be going? Von Kamp will probably return."

"He'll be back soon." Steve nodded at the suitcase. "Those are his clothes. I want to see him when he returns." He walked over and threw the bolt on the door, explaining, "I don't want him bursting in on us unexpectedly." He didn't add that he wanted time to get his gun before confronting their host.

"Am I a prisoner?" she asked, putting the wine aside.

"No, of course not." He put his hands on her arms. "It unlocks from the inside now. I just don't want Von Kamp coming in here and thinking we're burglars."

"Oh." She seemed disappointed.

"Or maybe I will hold you prisoner," he teased. He put his fingers under her chin and kissed her lightly. "We may be here a couple of hours. That's about as long as I can waste."

"Waste?"

"That was a bad choice of words."

He kissed her again.

"Girls in your country are this easy, aren't they?" she said.

"I don't know if 'easy' is the word anymore."

"You think I am."

"I think you're a beautiful, sensual girl, and I'm the lucky guy who's going to spend the next few hours with you."

"In bed, you think?"

"I don't know. I can't look that far ahead. Right now, I find it pleasant just to kiss you."

They stood, letting their senses get used to each other, letting their bodies stir at a slow, pleasant pace.

Eventually they were on a dusty couch and she had turned around so she lay on his lap while their lips grew hot and moist and his hands finally began wandering over the sleek white blouse she wore.

His own clothes were still somewhat damp, but she didn't seem to care.

She was not the aggressor, and she was slow to respond. When his hands finally moved to her bra-covered breast she held him off only for a moment before putting her hands on his shoulder and around his back where they wouldn't be tempted to interfere.

At no point was he certain she would yield; repeatedly her hesitation seemed determined. She stopped him for a while when he was unbuttoning her blouse, and she made him wait until she had her eyes closed. He didn't remove the blouse, just kissed her on the neck and down to her cleavage before he slipped a hand around to unfasten the bra. She didn't even make it easier by lifting herself, and he had difficulty getting the cloth cups off the small but smooth breasts that his hand finally reached.

Nor did she touch him, although she turned on her side, allowing him to swell to full size behind his zipper. But she did squirm gently against him while he undid the zipper on her skirt. By the time he had her skirt and half slip pushed awkwardly down her thighs and his fingers between her legs, she began to respond.

She rose, kissing him wildly and murmuring in Spanish. He couldn't translate quickly enough, but he understood.

Time to carry her to the bed.

He kept his lips on hers, felt her tongue probing his mouth as they approached the bed.

He had gone by the way of the door, switching off the lights before they lay together on the sheets. Her skirt and slip had fallen away, and he managed to get his own zipper and belt unfastened without letting her inhibitions surface. Her passion rose more slowly than he had ever known with any girl who wasn't obviously frigid.

"You don't know me," he heard her say in Spanish. She didn't think he could translate as much as he could or she wanted him to hear as she said, "My life was barren since I came home. Then you . . . you come out of nowhere. It isn't fair."

He wasn't sure he understood the last. It was of little importance anyway.

His biggest problem was getting his trousers off his legs without disrupting the growing flow of their need for each other.

He still had his shirt on as they lay in bed together. And his shorts.

He knew she was not bold enough to remove his shorts. In her mind it was a wanton act just for her to unbutton his shirt and shove it back off his shoulders as she did.

The shorts and panties still between them satisfied her sensitivities until demanding lust required their removal. After that she was a little more like the experienced girls he knew.

She could not allow herself to play anything except the passive role, but she did moan and cry out with pleasure instead of pain when he made his first tentative thrust. He went in cautiously, controlling himself for her sake.

Why?

She was more than a quick lay. Or rather it was more than a quick lay for her. She had been brought up in a more inhibited society than most of the girls he knew, and he had no desire to lessen her pleasure by wantonly violating her standards. He didn't judge her, just pleased her.

And while it was difficult to hold back, it extended the pleasure too.

Only when her hands finally joined together behind his back and brought him down and forward did he decide she was ready.

Ultimately she was wilder and more exciting than many women who had done it all. What the act lacked in ingenuity, it compensated for with that fresh, heart-thumping thrill of virginity lost.

And for a time they were wild. He climaxed just before she did, and she let herself go, pumping the last strength from his loins.

When it was over, he didn't roll aside and fall asleep, as nature insensitively designed most men to do. He stayed with her, holding and stroking her and whispering things that let her enjoy the part that was most important for her—the gentle afterplay.

And she rewarded him, kissing his chest and yielding when he encouraged her to move lower. It seemed like hours until she let his erection touch her cheek, days before she went farther. Experimentally she tried taking him in her mouth, withdrew, then tried again. It was something she had heard about at school, he guessed, and it took time for her to accept it. When she did, she became wildly passionate, forgetting any inhibitions she had ever had.

When it was over, she again lay in Steve's arms. Satiated, he again let her savor the aftermath.

He even restrained himself from looking at the luminous display of his digital watch.

He sat up only when he heard someone try the door from the outside.

The sound of the moving knob yanked him back into the world of reality, the world of people trapped in space, of men who tried to kill him, of links to dictators like Hitler and Perón.

Chapter 16

ANJELICA gathered up her clothes and ran to the bathroom. Steve settled for his shorts and gun, leaping to the door and freeing the latch. He could hear voices in the hall, and he had a moment to hide before the knob was tried again. He flattened his back against the wall. Instead of standing where the door would conceal him when it swung open, he chose the other side. There he waited with his gun in his left hand and his right poised just above the light switch.

The newcomers had better enter the way he expected.

He could hear the knob turning again.

Then the door flew open. The beam of a flashlight poked cautiously into the room. The holder stood directly on the other side of the wall from Steve, so the beam couldn't quite catch him. It swept across the room, hesitated on the closed entrance to the bath, and then concentrated on the space behind the hall door.

How many hundreds of films had shown someone hiding behind the door. The film cliché must have been as popular in Argentina as it was in the States.

No one spoke, but Steve could see a revolver in the beam and a hand reaching for the switch.

That's what he had hoped for.

He grabbed the wrist, hauled it down and forward in a two-man game of crack the whip. Startled, the figure lost its balance and was easily swung into the room, whirling and falling. Some hard and metallic object sailed through the air to bang against the far wall. The man's gun, Steve hoped.

Using the first man's weight as a counterbalance, Steve let go of his grip and went tumbling and rolling past the bed and behind the dresser.

The lights came on. There was a second visitor. A tall slender Argentine with mean eyes, the second man was caught blinking into the light, his gun pointed at his own partner.

"Freeze!" Steve yelled.

It didn't get translated fast enough. The guy swung his revolver.

Steve fired. Deliberately he missed. One shot as a warning.

There was no hero in the doorway. The Argentine dropped his gun and raised his hands. A man in his sixties was directly behind him.

Eric Von Kamp.

Steve recognized him from the pictures.

Breathing in deeply, savoring his satisfaction, Steve Crown was certain he had won. He had the man he had come to find. The rest would be easy.

"Come in, Mr. Von Kamp. I'm sort of a friend of your daughter's."

The former Nazi pushed aside the man in front of him and entered the room. He looked angry. There was no sense of the relief Steve thought he would feel.

"Who are you?" he asked.

"Steve Crown."

"What are you doing here?"

Steve saw the two men with Von Kamp estimating their chances. If both dove for their guns, surely one of them would live to kill the American.

"No good, boys," he said, hoping they understood English. "Before either of you gets to your gun, I'll kill Von Kamp."

One of them shrugged. "So, you kill him, we kill you."

The bathroom door opened, and Anjelica came out cautiously, dressed except for the shoes she carried in one hand. Her hair was a mess, though.

"*Mi Dios*," Anjelica gasped.

"Ah, now we have a girl to kill too." The man next to Von Kamp smiled. He spoke English very clearly.

"That bluff won't work," Steve said. "I don't give a damn about the girl and—"

"Steve!" Anjelica was shocked.

"—and I know your Nazi friend here is more important than your own lives to either one of you."

There was no response. He had guessed right, Steve decided. Whether they would have died for their cause or not didn't matter. Neither of the Argentines would lose his machismo image in front of the other, especially when complying meant they wouldn't have to risk their own lives.

"Get the two guns, Anjelica." He pointed them out to her on the floor.

"But you just said—"

"Do it."

She obeyed, looking rather ridiculous, a Latin aristocrat holding two pistols like a 1920s gun moll. She even swung the muzzles back and forth between Steve's captives.

Carefully Steve moved about the room, frisking all three men, including Von Kamp. None carried any more weapons.

Ordering the two gunmen to sit on the couch, he closed the hall door and began the awkward process of dressing without letting go of his snub-nosed revolver.

"All right, anybody care to explain this to me?" he said. "Or should I start trying to shoot off ears?"

Both men on the couch flinched. They took him seriously.

"I'm not a very good shot," he warned. "I mean, I'm not

bad. If I aim for an ear and miss, I'll get you straight through the eyeball instead, but I'm no grand national winner. So it's show-and-tell time. What's all this about?"

"Who are you?" Von Kamp asked.

"A friend of your daughter's," Steve repeated.

The older man's slumped shoulders straightened abruptly.

"She's all right?" he asked. His concern was genuine.

"Last time I heard." Steve nodded at the two men on the couch. "But apparently you're not doing too well. I take it these men and their friends are holding you prisoner."

"Prisoner?" All three echoed the word. They laughed.

"Señor Von Kamp is our friend," the tall spokesman for the two on the couch said.

Without warning, Steve fired. The bullet zapped past one man's ear and he reached up instinctively to see if it was still all there. Both men cried out.

"Es verdad, señor."

"Por favor. Señor Von Kamp is not our prisoner."

"Then what are the guns for?"

"To protect him, of course."

"From whom."

The Argentine frowned. *"No comprendo."*

"Oh, the hell you don't. Who are you protecting him from? Those two goons who chased me earlier today?"

"Goons?"

Anjelica translated for them.

"*Sí, sí*. It is from such people we protect our friend."

"Von Kamp?"

The answer was slow in coming and not entirely convincing. "They're telling the truth. I am not a prisoner."

"I don't believe it," Steve said. "I was at your home in Miami. There were two men and a girl there—all Spanish-speaking—searching the place."

"I am free to come and go."

"They burned your house," Steve said. He watched Von Kamp's eyes. The announcement shocked the older man, but he refused to respond. "I think they were trying to make it difficult to trace you by destroying any leads. Now you're here, between two Latin men with guns. That sounds like a kidnapping to me."

Von Kamp wasn't convincing as he said, "If you and the lady will leave, there will be no charges pressed against you."

"*Sí, amigo.*" The man on the couch stood. "Go. You are free to go."

"You're damned right I am. As long as I hold the gun. Now tell me the story. Why are they holding you, Mr. Von Kamp?"

"I told you, they aren't. I came down to sell this place. They are real estate agents."

"Real estate agents carrying guns? Bullshit!"

"It is dangerous in Argentina these days. We thought we would be carrying a great deal of money."

"Bullshit again. You don't conduct business as usual when your daughter is on a space shuttle. Space flights haven't become that common. And it's no coincidence that you're down here the day before she lands."

"The day before?"

Steve had touched a nerve that made all three men twitch.

"Yes, they're having problems."

"That changes nothing," Von Kamp said. "Please, whoever you are, just leave."

"If you're not a prisoner, then you're free to walk out of here with me and the girl," Steve said.

The pair on the couch exchanged glances with each other and then with the retired missile expert.

"But, of course, he is free to leave with you. If he wants."

"Which I do not."

Steve felt numb. He had assumed, if he found Von Kamp alive at all, he would be a prisoner, a hostage of some kind. Nothing else made sense. He ran through the possibilities quickly. If Von Kamp were a prisoner, he might easily deny it for a number of reasons, one being an attempt to let Steve and Anjelica escape. His captors might prefer to let the interlopers go, as long as it didn't appear they were breaking any laws.

"Doesn't matter," Steve said. "You're going with us to Buenos Aires."

"Don't be a fool."

"Go," one of the Argentines said magnanimously. "We will be here when you have convinced the *norteamericano*, señor."

"No."

"Steve, let's go," Anjelica pleaded. "I don't understand this but it seems you have made a mistake."

"Only one thing will convince me. You going with us, Von Kamp."

"Which I am not going to do."

"Then we go to plan B. This time I shoot your two friends."

"Don't be ridiculous."

"Steve!" Anjelica shouted.

He raised the gun and took aim at the taller of the two men.

Both men on the couch put their hands in front of them. *"No, por favor. Vaya, Señor Von Kamp."*

"All right, you stubborn idiot. If nothing else will convince you . . ."

He pivoted and walked to his suitcase. He repacked it quickly and started for the door. Steve backed after him. "Anjelica, get the picture."

She looked blank.

"The one in the middle."

He watched the two gunmen as she took the photo of Perón and Von Kamp's first wife from the chest of drawers. He swore he detected a flicker of concern in all four dark eyes.

The picture meant something.

He had Von Kamp.

And twenty-four hours before Shuttle Charlotte started her descent.

Angelica and Von Kamp went down ahead of him.

Confident he would soon have the truth from the astronaut's father, he rushed down the stairs, through the foyer, and out the front of the house. The two men whom he had disarmed followed casually. They didn't look concerned until he fired two shots, one into each front tire of the car parked out front.

They sat down, disgusted, perhaps thinking of the long walk to the main road.

They even waved and bade Von Kamp, *"Vaya con Dios,"*

watching wistfully as Steve led the way to the concealed Volkswagen.

Steve climbed into the rear seat of the VW with Anjelica at the wheel, Von Kamp next to her.

"Airport, Anjelica, fast," he said.

"But you said we couldn't fly at night. You . . ."

She stopped.

So, he thought. It's like telling your girl you ran out of gas.

Confidently, when they were away from the house and halfway to the airport, he leaned forward and said, "Okay, Mr. Von Kamp. You're free. Safe. Tell us what happened. What can I do to help?"

"You can let me go."

"No, you're flying out of here with us."

"Then you may release me in Buenos Aires so I can rejoin my friends."

"For Christ's sake, I spent the day—most of it, anyway—risking my life for you."

"You made a mistake. I am in no danger."

"Your daughter is. You called Houston and told them the bomb was aboard her craft."

"Not true."

"Not true, shit. They did a voice print. It was you calling."

Trapped in his lie, he was ready with an answer. "It was foolishness on my part. I . . . I didn't want her to go. Too dangerous. So I called, trying to stop her, but it seems I called after they had already taken off."

"I don't believe you."

"That is your problem, Mr. Crown. I'll be pleased if you will just release me in Buenos Aires."

Steve slumped back in his seat.

"Well, I'll be damned," he said.

Chapter 17

STEVE had watched a Torino, an Argentine-made car, swing in behind them as they left the mansion. He slowed, deliberately letting it catch up.

Tanya Horton was at the wheel.

He said nothing until they reached the airport at the hotel, then he motioned her forward and introduced her as his "assistant" to Eric Von Kamp.

Anjelica only nodded in recognition, and Steve could sense her drawing farther away from him. There was no use lying, no use trying to convince her that Tanya was at the falls by coincidence. And he couldn't tell her the truth. Any feeling between them had been killed.

He spoke to Tanya while he hustled the other two into the aircraft.

"Get someone to turn on the field lights," he told her. "You can fly back to Buenos Aires with us."

Tanya took the order with an impatient toss of her head, and simultaneously Anjelica Marcelo brushed away his helping hand. What had started out as a fling for her was turning mysterious and frightening. She sullenly climbed into the aircraft parked in the darkness along with the other private planes and small jetliners at the field.

Alone with Steve, Von Kamp had made another protest at being whisked off against his wishes.

"Unless you are kidnapping me, Mr. Crown," he said impatiently, "there is no sense in taking me any farther."

"They'd just take you to Buenos Aires, anyway." Steve fished for ideas.

"Why do you say that?"

"Because you're mixed up in Argentine politics," Steve guessed.

"I told you. I came to sell a house."

Steve wished he could see the old man's face more clearly.

"Don't tell me that house sat empty for decades without a reason."

Von Kamp sighed. "I bought the house for the Führer."

Steve cocked his head. "As his hideaway in case he lost the war?"

"No. The Führer never considered defeat." His voice fell as he recalled the old humiliation. "Yes, I suppose Hitler would have come here if he had survived. But he didn't."

"Why didn't you sell it if it was in your name?"

"Hitler's name was on some of the legal papers. Selling the property would have started people digging into the relationship of the Argentine government to the Nazis, causing a strain in relations with virtually every other country in the world. It was best forgotten."

"Why didn't the government just destroy the title papers?"

"A clerk, any low-level administrator might have noticed. As long as the records remain buried in the files, why chance it?"

"But you were going to sell it now."

"Yes, possibly. It has been so long."

"No, Von Kamp," Steve guessed again. "You weren't selling the house. It was used as a secret headquarters for Peronists."

"Don't be ridiculous."

"What I don't understand is why you came here when your daughter was going on a space mission."

"I came to sell the house. Nothing more."

"No."

"Believe what you like."

"When did you discover the actual plan? The bomb aboard the shuttle."

"There is no bomb."

"There is one, all right, and it's going off by nine o'clock tomorrow night at the latest." Steve checked his watch. It was long past midnight. "Christ, that's nine o'clock tonight."

Von Kamp's knees seemed to weaken. He put a hand to the fuselage of the aircraft to steady himself.

So soon, that's what he's thinking, Steve figured.

The former Nazi straightened his back.

"All this is foolish guesswork on your part."

"Is it?" Steve was forming a scenario in his mind. "Want me to suggest a possibility? You came down here because you know there's going to be a revolution by a group who won't give a damn about old connections between Argentina and Hitler—the Peronists. And that's somehow tied in with the space shuttle."

Tanya had returned. The lights of the field went on.

"There is no bomb." Von Kamp was firm. "Under no circumstances would I allow my daughter's life to be endangered."

He entered the aircraft, taking a place next to Anjelica in the rear.

"That I believe," Tanya said. "He may have been a Nazi at one time, but everybody says he's a good father."

"Shit! I'm getting nowhere. Maybe he's telling the truth."

Tanya shook her head. "I heard from your grandfather today. The astronauts jettisoned some of their gear to get closer to the suspected location of the explosives. They found a container next to the fuel cell."

"Aw, come on, don't tell me someone could get an unauthorized box aboard the spacecraft."

"No, there's supposed to be a container in that position, and there is. Right size. Right shape. Right everything except the part number. It's one digit off. The right container has been found on the shore off Vandenberg Air Force Base. Someone attempted to dispose of it in the sea. The only logical conclusion is that there is a destructive device aboard."

"And still no ransom demand?"

"None."

"But whoever put it there must want something."

Steve ran his hand over his weary eyes.

"Are you any closer to a solution?" she asked.

"No."

"You may be the only hope. The official investigation is bogged down."

"So am I. I swore Von Kamp was the key, but I haven't the slightest thread tying him to the bomb except his threat."

"I thought his son Domingo was involved. I would have sworn he was in hiding, but Roy found him at home, just as worried about his sister as any of us."

"And this is all I have for wasting a day and nearly getting myself killed." Steve showed her the photo taken from the dresser at the mansion.

"What's this?" she asked.

"A picture of Juan Perón and Domingo Von Kamp's mother. Wire it to my grandfather," Steve said, "the minute we get to Buenos Aires. I have a feeling it's been doctored."

"Doctored?"

"Changed, retouched or something."

"This is all we have? An old photograph?"

"And less than twenty-four hours," Steve answered as he opened the door and helped her into the plane. He checked his watch again. "Twenty hours and eleven minutes. We have our own countdown going now. A goddamned countdown to disaster."

Chapter 18

ROY Borden sat in the charter office, struggling through a magazine on aeronautical engineering, when the manager told him his friends had arrived.

He put the magazine aside and went out into the midmorning light.

He spotted Steve and Tanya, but he leaned against a wall, pretending not to recognize them until they went through the gate with the two companions who had accompanied them on their return flight from Iguassú Falls.

He followed, close enough to see Von Kamp walk to a taxi several yards away. The former missile expert had aged, judging from the pictures Roy had seen, but there was no mistaking him.

The only question was: Why was he being allowed to leave alone?

Steve and Tanya were ignoring Von Kamp, apparently warding off a verbal assault by a suave-looking gentleman.

"I don't believe it," Roy said to himself. Unless his Berlitz Spanish had failed him completely, Steve was being cursed by a father for keeping his daughter out all night. The girl—the one who had arrived with the two Counter Force agents moments before—had already been helped into the rear of a Mercedes limousine.

Roy recognized the father as the man who leaned to the window of the limousine and barked an order to the chauffeur.

Miguel Romonas Marcelo de Juárez, one of the two people in all Argentina who were supposed to help the Crown General Corporation team, watched his expensive car leave, then turned and snapped something more at Steve. With a shake of his fist, Marcelo turned toward the taxi stand.

Neither Steve nor Tanya moved as the aristocrat raised his hand and snapped his fingers.

From farther up the walk, four taxis tried to out-jockey each other. One snatched Eric Von Kamp from curbside, the other three tried for Marcelo. With the sixth sense of experienced cab drivers, all three spotted the expensive cut of his clothes. He talked briefly with the drivers, then selected one.

The fortunate driver closed the door graciously behind Marcelo and ran to his own place at the wheel. The taxi leaped from the curb like a sprinter answering the gun.

"Steve, Tanya," Roy said as he approached them.

Tanya Horton started to enter the nearest cab, but Steve confronted the remaining driver.

"Where did he say he was going?" Steve asked. "The rich one."

The driver looked stunned. *"Qué?"*

"Hable ingles?" Steve anxiously pressed the man's arm.

"Sí, sí, señor, hablo ingles muy bien."

"Yeah, I'll bet you speak Mandarin Chinese, too."

"Sí, señor, sí. Where you go?"

"The rich señor asks to be taken to Teatro Colon," the other driver answered.

"The opera?"

"Good God, Steve," Tanya cried. "What do you care where Marcelo is heading?" She pointed toward the first cab. "Von Kamp is getting away."

Steve turned then, wasting no time, not even to express surprise that Roy had popped up in Argentina.

"Roy, follow Von Kamp's cab. Get in touch with me at the Hotel California. Hurry!"

"Some welcome!" Roy grumbled. But he hailed another cab and jumped in the back seat.

He nudged the driver, pointed through the windshield, and said, "*Siga ese taxi, por favor. Pronto.*"

"Mister," cab driver said, "I speak English. We do more better in English. Okay?"

"Okay, follow that cab."

"It costs more, not to lose. Okay?"

"Yeah, yeah."

"Not to worry. You *norteamericanos* are lucky. In Argentina all of us go to university. Learn English. Study law. Much lawyers. No work. Thousands leave. Some stay. Drive taxis or autobus. Give great tours. You want to see the pink palace?"

"No, damn it, just keep your eyes on that cab."

Roy settled back in the seat.

He felt peevish, a small man's emotion that he rarely felt. But Steve hadn't even expressed surprise at his arrival, just sent him off on a private detective's job. It galled him. The whole shuttle bomb-scare show was narrowing down to a Steve Crown performance.

The FBI was scoring zero, so far as Adam Crown could determine. The CIA was being called in, but it would be tomorrow before they could get a man into Argentina. By then the shuttle would have landed—whole or in pieces.

And you haven't accomplished a damn thing, Roy berated himself.

Whether aware of it or not, Steve was the last hope for the astronauts. And more rode on Steve's shoulders than even the lives of four people. The entire space program was in jeopardy. A budget-cutting President and Congress would slice off huge hunks of NASA's civilian space program if the shuttle failed.

There was another danger, too: the responsibility could cross international borders. If the spacecraft were downed by agents of a second country (Cuba and half a dozen leftist regimes were already suspected), the President was in a mood to strike back. The people wouldn't stand by and watch their astronauts killed by terrorists.

Scuttlebutt had reached Roy that the Navy was already converging on Cuba.

And what was he doing? Following a cab like a $200-a-day private detective.

Roy fumed, then quickly cooled as reason returned to temper his anger. Steve was probably onto something big. He was probably right on track. He had to be. There was no other hope.

Tanya and Steve jumped into the last taxi.

"Hotel California," Steve snapped. That much the driver understood.

As the car swung out toward the expressway leading into the city, Tanya flung a question at Steve.

"How'd you know Roy would be at the airport?"

Steve had the photograph in his hands and was holding it to the light. "I didn't."

"Then why aren't we all following Von Kamp?"

"You think Roy needs someone to hold his hand?" He stared at the photo and shook his head.

"And why did you care where Miguel Marcelo was going?"

"That's a dumb question, woman," Steve exploded. "He's the one man in Argentina who is supposed to help us. I want to know where to find him if we need him."

"You screwed it up good with him, didn't you? Keeping his daughter out overnight, not even at a decent hotel. He'll never help us. That leaves Corpus Cristi."

"Cristi, hell! That bitch has tried to get me killed so often I'm losing count."

"But she works for us," Tanya protested.

"Sure, but whose side do you think she's on in the election? Is she rich? Is she one of the top two hundred families in Argentina? Hell, no."

"But that doesn't mean—"

"She went with me to the hotel. What happens? Bang, bang. The cops start playing cowboys and Indians. She leaps to my rescue. Nearly knocks me right into the gunfire."

"I didn't know about that."

"The same night she takes me to a cemetery and leaves me to get buried by the army. She charters me a plane—"

"You told her you were going to Iguassú?"

"No. But what's waiting for me up there? Two hit men who lead me to a perfect little place for an accident. If we hire one more agent like her to work for us, we'd better get six strong men as pallbearers."

"That does leave Marcelo."

"And I screwed that up. I'm lucky he doesn't come after me with a horsewhip. Then there's the girl. Anjelica. She thinks I used her."

"You did."

"I know. You think that makes me feel good?"

"My being there didn't help, did it?"

"I don't suppose it did."

"Sorry," she said.

He meant to express appreciation. Tanya's gun had saved his guts at the deserted house. But he was bent over his digital wristwatch, pushing at the buttons on the side.

"Now what on earth are you doing?" Tanya asked.

"Setting my alarm for nine P.M. After that it's all over, one way or another." He changed his mind. "Make it eight fifty-nine, forty-five."

"Why?"

"That gives me fifteen seconds to cover my ears and close my eyes."

"There'll be nothing to see or hear on earth," she said.

"But I'll feel it in my guts. That shuttle exploding or burning or . . ." He stopped. The taxi had slowed unexpectedly.

Several blocks back it had left the motorway and was now stalled by crowds moving on foot down the center of the street toward the heart of the city.

"Oh, no," Steve groaned. "It's already starting."

There was a more ominous sign, too. Trucks loaded with

armed soldiers rolled through the crowd behind a buttoned-up tank. People flung bottles at it or spat upon it.

There were police, too, hopelessly trying to prevent people from reaching the Avenida de Mayo. The avenue stretched from the docks through the heart of the city to the Plaza Congreso.

"The entire center of the city will fill with people by night," the driver said in Spanish, not attempting to fake English again. "The workers are calling a strike," Steve understood him to say. "I take you back to the airport. Okay?"

Steve glanced through the side window of the cab and saw police fighting with a half-dozen men carrying a great placard. It was printed on stiff cardboard and was apparently braced with wood on the back.

"Stop here," he snapped.

He tossed some bills at the driver and pulled Tanya into the open. They ran to the curb.

Steve dodged a police officer's baton only to get a glancing blow from one of the strikers. Although Argentina was a mixture of immigrant nationalities like the U.S., he and Tanya stood out as tourists.

He angered the workers as he pushed and shoved his way close enough to see the big placard clearly.

"Jesus Christ!" he murmured.

A fist caught his jaw, and a hand pushed him into the gutter. He didn't fight back.

"Steve, are you all right?" Tanya shouted, then swung her handbag to clear a space where she could help him to his feet.

He rose, ready to use his gun if necessary to make a path. Tanya's hand on his wrist made him reconsider.

He didn't understand the significance of what he had just seen, but he no longer doubted that he was onto a crucial lead. He couldn't allow anybody or anything to stop him.

"We're never going to get anywhere in a cab," he yelled over the noise.

"Perón, Perón, Perón," the people were beginning to chant.

A rock smashed the windshield of the taxi they had just left.

With the usual mentality of a mob, people squeezed in on

the vehicle, beating it with their fists, then kicking it and scratching the finish with whatever sharp objects they had in their pockets. Men were rocking it, attempting to upset it, while the driver tumbled about inside.

With attention diverted from them briefly, Steve and Tanya managed to drive a wedge through the milling mass of flesh.

When he had Tanya safe, Steve turned around, getting his bearings.

"Take that picture to the American embassy," he said. "Beg or threaten. But get it on the wire to Adam. Then go to the hotel and stay there. I'll keep calling until I get an answer from you."

"Why?" she asked. "Surely there's something I can be doing that's really connected with the shuttle."

"I think it is. I'm positive it is."

"What makes the picture so important?"

"I don't know."

"But you're more certain than ever since you looked at that big placard."

"Look around you. Dozens of people are carrying those placards. By night they're going to be plastered all over the city."

"So? What do we care? We have our own national emergency."

"Yeah. Right here. If that space shuttle is saved, it's going to be done right here in Argentina. Don't ask how. I don't know, but this is where it happens. Those placards prove it. For me, anyway. They're blowups of the picture I gave you. Domingo Von Kamp's mother with Juan Perón."

"I still don't see—"

"Neither do I, but there's something out of kilter in that picture. Just do as you're told," he ordered irritably.

Normally she would have lashed out at him, refused to take his orders. He wasn't her boss. Adam Crown was. Steve worked as a team member or she didn't work with him at all.

But today Steve was different.

He shouted his order—treated her as he had treated Roy at the airport—then plunged into the crowd and was gone.

"Damn you, damn you, Steve Crown. You chauvinistic

pig." With venom lanced by her outburst, she looked at the photograph. She had no choice.

She turned sideways, the photograph in her purse protected by her left arm, her right elbow now a weapon she could use to dig her way through the crowd.

Chapter 19

ADAM Crown scanned the fourth copy of the photograph. The federal agents in Washington had the first copy and were having it studied by experts. Another had gone to Houston, where it was beamed via television to the space shuttle.

A third stayed in the San Diego offices of the FBI, and the fourth was rushed to the Crown mansion.

Adam clutched it as he might a prized memento. Time was ticking away fast. The minds of hundreds were stuck on the problem of saving the shuttle, and he felt personally frustrated with the case. Normally he was in the midst of the action when his private force went on the offensive, but circumstances had left him on the outskirts—mainly because he didn't know where the real action was.

Perhaps his grandson was right. Maybe something vital to saving the spacecraft was occurring in Argentina. But Adam doubted it. Maybe it was Houston, but things seemed normal there. The preparation for reentry was being conducted as routine.

And in Washington the government was flailing about with meaningless activity and a minimum of words. Preparations had begun for television coverage of the craft's return even while debates raged in a tight circle around the President.

When to announce the true predicament about Shuttle Charlotte: that was the question.

The President procrastinated, standing at the window of the Oval Office and looking out at the snow-covered gardens, his icy fury confined in silence. He feared he might overreact where astronauts were concerned. They held a special grip on the minds and emotions of the nation, himself included.

He *knew* he would overreact; the consequences would be staggering, but the overwhelming frustrations of his office had finally been too heavily spiced with this one particularly sadistic threat of terror.

Anybody, any group, any nation responsible would choke on its own fanaticism if the astronauts died. Yet the prospect of vengeance was no help. Waiting, watching the clock was torture.

In his San Diego mansion, Adam Crown, at least, had work to do. He could study the photograph and determine if something was amiss, as his grandson suspected.

Expecting a long session, he settled at his conference-room table, a magnifying glass in one hand, a bottle of vodka and snacks to his side, and his other hand holding the enlargement flat to the mahogany surface.

He leaned close, took a sweeping overall view, then stopped almost immediately with the glass magnifying the pack of cigarettes on the table near Juan Perón. After holding there briefly, the glass moved to the other item that had caught his attention: the calendar.

1944.

"Damn!" He swore with disappointment. He didn't need experts. He had his answer.

Reaching for his telephone, he dialed a room at the Hotel California in Buenos Aires. Although he anticipated a delay, considering the situation in the troubled capitol, the automated worldwide direct dialing system worked perfectly. And Tanya was waiting for the call as directed.

"The photograph is a fake," he told her without so much as a hello. Holding the picture in front of him, he said, "It is a composite—parts of two different photographs butted together and retouched."

"Washington gave you an answer that fast?" she responded.

"An old man does not need an expert in this case. Nothing except his own memory. Lucky Strike green went to war before '44."

"What?"

"You are too young to know, but do you have the photograph before you?"

"Yes."

"Do you see the Lucky Strike cigarette package?"

"Yes."

"It appears in the black and white picture to be predominantly a dark-colored pack."

"True."

"Lucky Strike packages were predominantly green until shortly after the war began. Then they changed the package to white outside the circle. They had a slogan that became a household phrase—one of the great advertising slogans of all times. 'Lucky Strike green has gone to war.'"

"What does that mean?"

He smiled, remembering the patriotism of a major war. "I don't think anyone knew except the advertising agency. I always thought it meant they were saving green ink to help the war effort."

"So the package dates the left hand of the picture with Perón in it, presuming the cigarettes were not several years old."

"A safe assumption, I believe."

"And the calendar dates the right-hand side of the picture. 1944."

"Yes."

"Meaning Perón and Von Kamp's first wife were not photographed together."

"Someone, sometime, wanted to give the impression that they had been together. Wait," he said. "My other phone is flashing."

He put Tanya's call on hold and picked up another telephone. A voice spoke to him from Washington without identifying itself. "You're right. The picture is a composite. The two originals were taken with different negative film, and there are signs of retouching—extremely well done, but apparently done recently, using techniques not known until the last five to ten years. What does it mean?"

"I don't know. Possibly something very important in Argentina and possibly related to our spacecraft troubles. If I am able to make any sense of all this, I will get back to you." He hung up and spoke to Tanya again. "I have confirmation. Tell the boy—"

"You mean Steve?"

"Tell the boy to proceed on the assumption that the photograph has been faked, and insist he tell me what he thinks that means."

"I'll try. But I can tell you this. The people are tacking up poster-sized blowups of that picture all over the city, faster than the police can tear them down."

"Interesting," Adam Crown said. "Very interesting. I think"—his fingers drummed the table—"I should be there."

"You would have difficulty getting to Argentina in time," Tanya said.

"And where is the boy now?"

"I don't know."

"You don't know! We have become the plow and the farmer. We have a vast field, but we don't know where to find the horse. Doesn't he know how little time is left?"

"He knows," Tanya said. "He knows."

Steve Crown let himself be pushed along by the crowd through unlit streets; the power had failed or been turned off by the authorities to hamper the demonstrators. He had gotten nowhere until he took to the subway. No trains were running. And hundreds of people had the same idea. They were walking through the empty tunnels, their matches, cigarette lighters, and occasional flashlights providing the only aid as they moved along, each keeping one hand on the wall for guidance.

The dark caverns were a nightmare.

Like ghouls, the thieves and bullies formed a gauntlet. Steve heard cries ahead in the dark. Men were being mugged by unseen hands. Women were being raped. The sadistic laughter of thieves and rapists made the black cave a gruesome carnival attraction.

When hands reached for Steve Crown's wallet, though, the attached but invisible body got a painful shock. Steve swung his arm until he found a neck, then his strong hands crushed together snapping bone and flung the gagging ghost aside.

More muggers formed a shoulder-to-shoulder line across the tunnel, holding back the stumbling crowd until Steve reached it. Standing sideways, he kicked knee high. He felt a kneecap slip out of position and heard a man cry in agony.

At neck height he held his palm flat, fingers fused, the arm cocked at the elbow. With the power of a machine ejecting clay pigeons for trapshooters, his arm uncocked. It smashed flesh and bone. He heard a grunt from the right. Using his left in a similar fashion, he caught another thief across the temple. The blow hurt Steve's hand, but the two unconscious bodies that bumped against him as they fell gave him satisfaction.

The band of hoodlums who preyed on the innocent in the darkness suddenly found the lack of light to be both ally and enemy. They couldn't tell what was happening. Some unseen force was chopping their number like a lumberjack felling saplings.

They gave way to yelling at each other. Sightless, more terrified than their intended victims, the vultures suffered panic of their own making.

"*Vamos*," Steve yelled to the crowd.

Hundreds surged forward. The line fell and was trampled unmercifully. Steve was acting on a hunch: the head of the crowd would point like an arrow to his target. At the tip he would find what he was seeking—the quarry, the salvation of the shuttle.

It was his last hope.

Where the crowd left the tunnel, Steve followed to a boulevard. Here the lights in the streets and some of the buildings worked, and here the demonstrators stopped and settled in.

It had taken hours to reach the boulevard, and the people were exhausted from the crush. Most took to sitting down, claiming a bit of turf or pavement for themselves. The more limber climbed into trees or sat on the few cars that had been left on the avenue. Everyone looked toward a single building.

It was nondescript except that, unlike the stores and most other structures in the surrounding area, the display windows were neither caged nor boarded up against potential vandals and looters.

Among the crowd, fights ignited. Men went at each other with broken bottles as weapons. The bleeding crept away, the victorious claimed prime turf.

Groups of toughs decided they wanted the best perches and took to shaking the trees until the first occupants tumbled down, twisting limbs and breaking bones. Vicious king-of-the-hill battles were fought for the tops of cars.

"What's happening?" Steve tried to ask people around him. *"Qué pasa?"* If anyone understood him, no one replied, and the hostile gazes people returned encouraged him to keep moving. Stepping over arms and legs, he wormed his way forward.

He preferred to be deep inside the crowd. The police and army troops were leisurely arresting those on the fringes of the vast mob. It was being done as if it was an everyday occurrence.

Only an occasional demonstrator resisted, and he was quickly beaten into submission. Clubs used on faces crushed cheeks and caused a great deal of bleeding.

Obviously the police wanted to instill maximum fear with the maximum visual effect.

Their system worked.

Most of the demonstrators refused to go to the aid of their compatriots. They were not dedicated enough to the cause to risk the wrath of the police, and the government apparently was not yet convinced that the threat was serious enough to warrant full assault.

Most coup attempts failed or were settled with a few threatening shots. South American military men and politicans had a keen sense of public opinion and knew when to fight and when to flee.

Besides, it was the wrong season. The summer heat normally weakened the masses. While in the States summer was often an excuse for looting, the Argentines had been dragged from their siestas and were cranky, directing their ill tempers as much at each other as at the army troops.

Steve, though, kept working his way forward.

At the wall of men in white shirts, with their sleeves rolled up like laborers and with black mourning bands on their upper left arms, he was halted by the guards charged with holding back the masses.

"I have to get in," he tried to argue. "Do you speak English?"

The men cursed him and pushed him back.

He tried another angle, flashing his California fishing license with all of its stamps as identification. "CIA. *Estados Unidos. Sus amigo. Comprende?*"

Immediately a conference began, the guards demanding more and more identification from his wallet.

Just when it seemed hopeless, Roy Borden appeared from inside the building. Spotting Steve, he came over, mumbled a few unintelligible words, and took his friend's arm.

"How the hell did you get in?" Steve asked.

"I followed Von Kamp. They let him in right away, but when I told the guards I was with him, they started to attack me. Fortunately Corpus Cristi was here and knew me by name."

"Cristi, that bitch."

"*Buenos noches, Señor Crown*," Cristi said pleasantly as she came to the line of the guards.

"You're one of them, you bitch!" Steve grumbled.

The Argentine's eyes expressed hurt. "One of the Peronistas? But of course. I am *simpático* with them, at least. I am a worker in a land ruled by the rich and the military."

Steve's hand inched toward his gun. "Then you admit you tried to have me killed, here and at the falls."

"Are you here to meddle in Argentine politics?"

"Hell, no."

"Then why should I try to have you killed?"

"Because I caught up to Eric Von Kamp."

"I still do not understand. Señor Von Kamp is a guest."

"Why?"

Cristi frowned. "I don't know. Ask him yourself." She held out her hand to make way for Steve to enter.

"You'll take me to your leader, too?"

She laughed. "Leader. We have no leader. That is the problem, don't you see? We have no Perón."

Steve didn't believe that. "Somebody organized all this."

"Some members of the party get telephone calls. Do this. Do that. Who calls, no one knows. The party is outlawed. To be a leader would be fatal."

"And you get calls?" Steve asked.

"Today, yes. Never before. I am a nobody in the party. I have no time for politics. But today I am told, come here. So I come."

"We hired you," Steve barked. "Promised to pay you well. Now this."

"You pay me to help you find Señor Von Kamp? No?"

Steve hesitated. He couldn't remember precisely how much he had told Corpus Cristi. It didn't matter anymore.

"I found him on my own," he admitted. "But I want to see him again."

"Good. Then I take you to him. Come."

"I'm not going into that mess defenseless," Steve said. "I'm armed."

"So is everybody. Come, if you like."

Steve hesitated. It was a trap, he figured. But Roy had been inside. And he was walking opposite Corpus Cristi, making a way through the cordon of guards.

Warily, Steve Crown stepped across the imaginary line and into the inner circle of the revolutionaries.

"I will say you are journalists," Cristi said. "Pretend to take notes. Every Peronista wants the world to know what they are trying to do."

"What is this place?" Steve looked up at the sign above the

entrance of the building. "Radio and television studios?"

"There are transmitters on the roof," Roy told him.

Momentarily, neither of them spoke. A transmitter. Just what was needed to set off an explosion device aboard the shuttle. Steve's heart thumped in his chest. He was there. He was in the place where it was going to happen.

Somebody had a button they were going to push.

But how was he going to stop him—or her?

"Should have guessed it." He tried to sound casual. Roy must know too. "One of the first places revolutionaries capture these days. A means to reach the people. But why hasn't the government turned off the power?"

"The station has standby generators, I imagine," Roy suggested. He dropped back behind Cristi long enough to whisper, "We haven't a prayer of knocking out the transmitter, the studio, the antennas, or the generators. They're guarded tighter than Air Force One."

Steve cautiously followed Cristi and Roy into the building.

The ground floor consisted of nothing except tiled floor, banks of elevators, a security guard's desk, windows in front, and a dry fountain with a futuristic piece of stainless steel twisted together in a design format that would match a psychologist's ink blot test.

Guards in work clothes stood at each elevator with automatic rifles slung over their shoulders. When confronted with the two Americans, they swung their weapons menacingly until Cristi said the right words.

"*Tres*," Cristi told the boy operating the automatic elevator.

"Three. Is that where the action is?" Steve asked Roy.

"Yes. That's where Von Kamp went when Cristi brought me in. I watched the floor indicator after the old man entered the elevator. There was no chance of riding with him."

The elevator stopped on three and their guide stepped ahead of them to clear their presence with a guard.

"Anything interesting about this floor?" Steve asked.

"Yeah, note this. You can see through windows into the studio and the transmission equipment."

"So?"

"There's not a damn soul in there. The station is on full

automatic. There's not even an engineer inside. Maybe outside, but not in."

"But the station is operating?"

"Radio and TV. They've got monitors outside. The radio is broadcasting street sounds. So is the TV channel."

"With what picture?" Steve asked.

"A shot of the balcony outside this floor."

"So there'll be people speaking from the balcony."

"Undoubtedly. And their speeches will be transmitted to all Argentina. All automatically. Nothing, nobody we can get at."

"What's Cristi doing?" Steve asked when they had left the elevator and entered the crowded third floor.

"Same as me. She says all she was told to do was let us in. Anybody from Crown General."

"Oh, fuck."

"What's wrong?"

"Somebody wants us here. Either they're going to kill us or they have a reason. We'll be told to do something—or refrain from doing something to save the shuttle. Something we won't like."

"But Von Kamp came here. They greeted him as though he were the reincarnation of Perón."

"The people who met him—they didn't call him Perón, did they?"

"No, they used his own name."

"Then you couldn't expect the people to believe he's the reincarnation."

They walked into a large carpeted area of identical desks with private offices along the walls and to the front. Most of the floor was filled with men, five-gallon cans of gasoline, empty bottles, and old rags. They were preparing Molotov cocktails for the expected battle. Other men were loading rifles and handguns.

"Wait here," Cristi said. "I will try to find Von Kamp for you."

When she was gone, Steve picked up a phone, found it still working, and dialed the hotel.

Tanya Horton came on the line.

"You guessed it," she said. "The picture is a fake. Perón

and the actress were not together. What's it mean?"

"I don't know," Steve said. "I'll be damned if I know. But I have the feeling I've been suckered into the wrong place at the right time."

Chapter 20

ABOARD the space shuttle, the commander watched as Charlotte Von Kamp came through the airlock and removed her pressurized suit. When she had her helmet off, she shook her head sadly.

The men turned back to their instruments and their private thoughts.

She had been one last hope. They had sent her into the cargo area to see if her smaller hands could manipulate the tools needed to remove the container suspected of holding the bomb.

She too had failed.

Commander James Carlyle took a deep breath and spoke into the scrambler mike.

"Mission Control, this is Shuttle Charlotte. We have a negative on last instructions. Device still remains in place. Got any other bright ideas?"

On the ground in Houston, Mission Control director Fred Yarkin cleared his throat.

"Sorry, Jim. That was the last suggestion we had."

"Anybody on the ground working on any good preventive measures?"

"Hell, yes." Yarkin put as much reassurance in his voice as he could. "The FBI is all over this thing. A man responsible for the final inspection of that area of the shuttle was apprehended trying to cross into Canada. He claims he thought the cylinder contained letters."

"Letters?"

"Yes, for stamp collectors. He was to get a cut from the sale of the first shuttle mail."

"The bastard."

"He's cooperating, but everything was arranged by phone."

"Anything else?"

"State and local police are checking out every ham operator capable of sending a signal. And here in Vandenberg—"

"Fred, cut the horseshit. We've only got one more orbit left. Anybody, anywhere along our course—on the ground or airborne—can detonate that bomb with the right beep on the right frequency. You could arrest every ham and citizen band operator in the U.S. and still not guarantee us shit."

Yarkin inhaled and exhaled slowly.

"Affirmative, Jim. Sorry."

The voice from space reeked with futility.

"Then get our wives and kids. We'd like to say good-bye."

"Not good-bye, Jim. There's still hope."

"Yeah, well, get them anyway." James Carlyle looked back at Charlotte. "What about you, kid. Got a boyfriend you want to talk to?"

"Any chance of reaching my father?"

"You hear that, Mission Control?"

"Yes, but I'm afraid your father's out of contact."

"My brother, then."

"Okay, we'll get him on the line as soon as we can track

him down. Stand by, fellows. I'll have your families on the line in a minute. Tell them whatever you want."

Carlyle surveyed his crew again. "I say we tell them the truth this time."

"Our families? Tell them we're going to die?" Arnold Dumas said incredulously.

"Got nobody to tell," the pilot Alex Bunyan said softly, "except a girlfriend who really doesn't give a damn."

Arnold Dumas shook his head. "Oh, I don't know. Maybe you can, Jim, but me . . ."

"It's all of us or none, Arnold. They'd tell each other. So, I guess it's up to you. Sort of a veto power."

Arnold stiffened his jaw and said, "Okay, it's a go on the truth. God, that's going to be hard. Like an execution."

"That settles it."

James Carlyle looked down at the earth. An earth he'd never touch again.

"Coming over the south pole," Alex Bunyan said. "Next landfall will be over Buenos Aires. And when we pass over Argentina again we'll be hitting the buttons for our descent."

"Nine P.M. Buenos Aires time," Charlotte calculated. "Do you suppose anyone down there will see the flash?"

"Christ, Charlotte, don't think that way," Arnold said.

"Sorry."

"It must be your goddamned Nazi father," Alex Bunyan exploded. "He put the fuckin' bomb there and then warned us so we'd have hours to suffer. If it weren't for you . . ."

Charlotte paled.

James Carlyle barked at him, "Stop it, Alex."

"Is that what you're all thinking?" Charlotte cried. "That my father's responsible?"

"Or maybe your brother," Alex said viciously.

"You could ask your brother outright, if they find him," Arnold Dumas said.

"It couldn't hurt to ask," James Carlyle said with control.

"No. Mission Control would think I suspect one of them," she said.

Alex exploded again. "The whole world's going to suspect

them sooner or later. After our ashes sprinkle down like black rain. So talk to them."

The radio crackled and Fred Yarkin's voice returned to the speaker.

"Shuttle Charlotte, this is Mission Control. We have your families standing by. Sorry, Charlotte, we haven't found either your brother or father yet. And you, Alex, no next of kin?"

"No next of kin!" Alex said. Then he looked at Charlotte. "It is one of them."

"Shut up," Carlyle demanded. He flicked the mike on. "Put my wife on first, Fred."

"Right, Commander. Stand by."

"Aw, God," Arnold Dumas sighed. "How the hell am I ever going to tell the kids?"

Alex settled back, then turned and put a hand on Charlotte's. "Sorry, kid. I'm talking crazy. Want to go downstairs?"

"Downstairs? Why?"

"You know—what we talked about. A historic first in space."

"I couldn't. I . . ."

Alex had left his seat and was pulling himself through the air above her.

"Come on."

He unfastened her belt for her. "We're going to die," she said from a daze.

Alex grinned. "Yeah, and this is the only way to go," he said.

Chapter 21

A flight of jet fighters screamed out of the sky, dipped low between the towering skyscrapers, and created panic in the crowded streets before climbing in a sharp, steep turn.

"Bombs," people shouted in Spanish.

"Machine guns."

"Watch out."

Thousands of spectators rose in unison. Those on the fringes fell back easily. Those in trees or on top of cars jumped in an attempt to escape, knocking others to the pavement. Many started running. The old and the infirm were trampled. The wail of pain and fear replaced the blast of the jets.

A complete stampede was averted only by a voice booming from loudspeakers on the broadcast building balcony.

"Remain calm. They will not hurt you."

A few were badly injured in the crush of moving bodies. Friends and relatives crowded around. Spectators raised on their toes for a look at the blood. The most seriously injured were raised overhead and passed from hand to hand toward the edge of the crowd.

The loudspeaker boomed again.

"The whole world is watching. The soldiers won't dare hurt you. This I promise you."

Another flight of aircraft zoomed threateningly low over the people. The planes darted in and out like bats diving on insects in the pools of light under street lamps.

Few in the street could resist the urge to duck their heads and hunch their shoulders.

"The whole world is with us. The United States is with us," the voice said.

The United States?

That came as a shock. No revolutionary in the people's memories had ever claimed American assistance before.

The United States had always been the villain blamed by successive politicians for every conceivable problem they failed to solve. But tonight the words were magic. It gave the people the courage of vast armies and nuclear weapons.

Now the people conjured the mighty strength of the North Americans coming to their aid against the military junta, against the rich and powerful.

When the third wave of planes swooped in, the people stood tall. Someone started to sing "Himno Nacional Argentino," the national anthem.

They sang louder and with more robust pride when the planes made a fourth pass.

The air force scare tactics had always worked before. The military could roll a few tanks into the capital and swoop in with jets. The people had always fled in terror.

From the upper floor of a tall building just beyond the edge of the crowd, generals watched in amazement. The laborers had courage, an inner strength not tested since the days of Perón.

One bomb, a few bullets might send them scurrying, or it

might break the dam of carefully constructed fear. That fear had enabled a few determined men to keep the masses walled in for decades.

"Order the attack," one general said.

"Now," said another.

A third was more cautious. "Let them tire first. They might overrun us now."

"The troops might join the mob."

"Wait. They have no leader."

"Not yet."

Wait. That was the consensus.

And in the street, the people were chanting again.

"Perón, Perón."

"Resurreccion Perón. Viva Perón. Perón."

"Perón, Perón."

"Resurreccion. Perón. Viva Perón. Perón."

Inside the broadcast building, Steve Crown and Roy Borden had run to an open window when they heard the jets roaring over the city.

Armed revolutionaries and newsmen from around the world pressed close to the windows too—some fearful, some merely impressed with the noise of the aircraft.

"God!" Steve exclaimed. "Do you think the government will bomb the crowd?"

"Never," an American reporter said with a smug grin. "This is nothing but a media event. Staged by both sides."

Steve turned and faced him, silently asking for more of his opinion.

"The Peronists are a dying breed. Like the American Nazi Party," the reporter went on. "Their leader died years ago."

"The American Nazi Party never draws a crowd like this," Roy observed.

"The U.S. isn't in such rotten shape as Argentina, either. Besides, the Peronists promised a resurrection. Who wouldn't come to see that?"

"But why does the government allow it? They stomp out any other opposition."

"Because the Peronists are digging their own grave. What can they do for the big show—the 'Resurrection'? Nothing.

Show Evita's corpse. That's all they have. The people will take one morbid look—they think of death differently than we do—then they'll go home and talk of Saint Evita. Millions revere her, but they're not stupid enough to follow a corpse."

Unconvinced, Steve pushed away from the window. Nobody could predict what a mob would do.

The junta might be making a mistake by allowing the laborers to vent their protests and have their glimpse of the revered corpse. But the military men must know their people best.

They would probably make a few arrests, use tear gas, fire a volley of shots when the crowd was dispersing anyway—make a show of force. Perhaps even use the demonstrations as an excuse to call off the pending elections.

"None of this helps us," Roy Borden said as they retreated to the quiet of an empty office. "It doesn't save the shuttle. Damn it, Steve, I'm afraid you've finally driven us down the wrong alley."

Steve grunted. "I think you're right." He looked at his watch. "Christ, it's eight-twenty."

"The resurrection is at eight-thirty."

"To hell with that. The shuttle starts down at nine. And I have a hunch it'll blow right on the dot. Drama. That's what a maniac wants, so he'll go for the exact stroke of the hour." Steve had picked up the phone to call Tanya. "He'd kill on the stroke of midnight if he could."

"He?" Roy said. "No. This isn't one maniac we're looking for. This is a group. It took years of planning, carefully cultivated connections throughout the American aerospace industry, skill, and mechanical know-how to get that bomb aboard. The entire plot was masterminded by a knowledgeable politician or organizer, one too smart to think he could win a rebellion behind a corpse."

"The Argentine government thought it could be done."

"When?"

"Years ago, when Evita first died. They rushed her body out of the country and hid it for years for fear the Peronists could rally a coup behind the dead Evita."

"That was long ago. When she was first dead. When devotion to her was running high."

Steve stared at his friend.

Roy was right. Someone smart had to be running the show if the shuttle was tied in to the revolt.

But who?

And how, and why?

And what else was planned?

"Steve, listen!" Roy said, clutching at his friend's arm.

The sound came from outside. The crowd was cheering more wildly than ever. The pair returned to the window. Flood lamps lit the balcony, where someone stood at the railing, arms outstretched.

Neither recognized the figure.

"Who the hell is that?" Steve asked of no one in particular.

"A political nobody," an American journalist answered. "A popular actor. The Peronists must have hired him to start the show."

"Or to keep secret the identity of the real leader," Corpus Cristi volunteered. She had come up beside them and motioned to a desk where a telephone lay beside the cradle. "For you, Don Steve."

"A telephone call now?" He scooped up the phone. "Yeah?"

Tanya spoke in his own tone of voice. "I checked," she said. "And covering them all is impossible."

"What are you talking about? Damn it, Tanya. The lid's about to blow here. How'd you find me?"

She ignored the question. With the massive crowd out front, it couldn't have been difficult to figure where he would try to be.

"There are two hundred fifty-five radio and twenty-five television stations in the country. All censored, none guarded. Any one of them could be rigged to transmit a signal to the shuttle."

"All right, all right. It doesn't matter. I'm already at the right one, I'm sure."

"Not to mention sound trucks, mobile TV units, broadcast points like the Teatro Colon, several private studios, radio hams, police and military communications networks, and their equivalent of our citizen band radios. Probably everything except the CBs could transmit a strong enough signal straight up to reach the shuttle."

"Forget it. I gotta go."

"Wait, there's something more. I asked Charlotte Von Kamp what pictures her father had in his den. Remember you told me to ask?"

"Yeah, I remember."

"Nothing unusual. Just family pictures."

"Including his son and first wife?" Steve asked.

"Yes."

"Then those were the two missing pictures," he shouted with uncontrolled enthusiasm. "Somebody, a Peronist I'll bet, wanted as few pictures as possible around that showed Domingo and his mother. Maybe they thought that would slow down our search."

He was living in hopes that any new piece of information would finally lead him to a solution. That's how he operated.

Domingo Von Kamp and Maria Gallardo. The pictures had been taken and the house burned to wipe away as many memories of the two as possible.

Then suddenly Steve thought he knew why. He just wasn't positive yet.

Tanya asked, "What do I do now? I can't get through the crowd."

"I don't know. Talk some soldier out of his grenades."

"Talk?"

"Shoot him. I don't care. Just set off a diversion. Give me time to figure out what's going on." He dropped the phone on the cradle and turned around.

Hearing the crowd without distraction again bothered him. Were all those people out there his enemies? Nice, gentle, decent people, probably. But now . . .

"God, Roy," he groaned. "What makes people turn into a mob?"

"Envy," Cristi said. "The poor can accept poverty. It is seeing the rich that drives them to revolt. They prefer that all should starve rather than leave a few alive to feast."

"That's not our fight," Steve insisted. "Unless this ties in with our mission."

"So what do you suggest?"

"Go upstairs. Close down the radio-TV transmitters here and pray to God they were the ones to be used in blasting the shuttle."

"No!" Corpus Cristi said. "I couldn't allow that."

"You're supposed to be on our side," Steve reminded her.

"Against my own people?"

"It doesn't matter," Roy said. "They'll have backups. Close this one down and they'll broadcast the detonate signal from another station."

"At the last minute then. A few seconds before nine, we close her down. We can shoot up the whole damned station if we have to. We won't give them a chance to use another, and if the shuttle can keep a fuel cell working through the first seconds of reentry, they can get the rest of the way down using the hydraulic backup system."

"I do not understand," Cristi said.

"All we have to do is keep the ship intact until nine," Steve said.

"What makes you so sure they'll wait until the last second? It might already have gone off." Roy considered his own question and checked his watch. Thirty-three minutes to go. "Steve, it would be suicide. There's not a chance of getting at those transmitters."

Steve took a moment to admit the impossible. He'd never get through the fanatic guards to stop a signal from being sent. Even Cristi was against him.

Revolutionaries in their shirt sleeves, all carrying guns, crowded the floor.

The name Perón was all this one segment of the population had to bind them together, to give them hope, to remind them of days when their kind had ruled.

The entire room was filled with shouting men and women. If there was organization, Steve couldn't comprehend it. Most of the people were in the main bay, which held a hundred desks in lines, all facing the same direction, each with a typewriter, telephone, calendar pad, and stacked in-and-out mail trays. It seemed to symbolize the regimentation of the entire working class.

The elevators opened in ten- to twenty-second intervals, dumping off one load of sweating men and women with hard, set mouths and then scooping up another load to take them elsewhere in the building.

Then, as Steve watched, the elevator routine changed. Suddenly burly men held open one door, and began to shout, "Evita, Evita, Evita, Evita!"

Steve twisted around. He didn't believe what he was seeing.

Men were carrying a coffin from the elevator. The face of Evita Perón stared up through the transparent lid.

Men kissed the coffin. Women fell down on their knees and touched their foreheads to the floor. People wept as it was carried past. Dozens fell in behind it.

So did Steve, following as it was taken into a large conference room which opened onto the balcony and into the street below.

"Evita!" the people in the street screamed. "Evita!"

And suddenly he understood the cult of the Peronists.

She had been one of their own, a commoner raised in a land controlled for generations by the top two hundred families.

She had risen through sheer determination to stardom in radio and films. Then she had become the mistress and finally the wife of Juan Perón, the Argentine president who had promised the masses a better life.

And for a time he and his Eva had delivered.

Evita went among the workers, heard their pleas, and returned to the pink presidential palace. Her husband listened and ordered pay raises—twenty percent, twenty-five, thirty. Businessmen who resisted had their properties confiscated or they simply disappeared.

With her fragile little body she humiliated the smug society leaders the way the masses had wanted to do for generations. She could wear ermine, but the people adored her. She kept her promises to them.

To her grave.

She had given them hope, and now on the balcony a ritual

was being performed with the body of the illegitimate peasant child. Her coffin was being lowered with ropes and pullies to the sidewalk in front of the building.

She was going to lie in state again.

Thousands were crushing each other for a view. And Steve too forced himself forward until he could at least see onto the balcony.

The excitement, the adulation were beyond his comprehension, but then he had not seen what she had done for her people to rate such reverence.

The excitement faded rapidly.

Even as the actor and half a dozen others were trying to rouse the crowd to a new frenzy, the mob was being encouraged to express disappointment.

The shouting was unorganized. It was not military propaganda spokesmen casting doubts on the miracle. The protests were coming from within the crowd itself. Some were crying in the front row; others were protesting from farther away.

With little resistance, several men took control of the microphone on the balcony.

Steve could catch only bits and pieces of what these people were saying.

"No es verdad."

"No . . . resurreccion."

"Mentioso."

"Falsario!"

Liar, faker. They were not accepting Evita's embalmed body as the resurrection they had been promised.

"Perón, Perón, Perón, Perón!"

The chanting began, but it was a threatening drumbeat preparing the people to storm the building.

Steve backed from the conference room. If the crowd charged the building, there might be no worry about smashing the transmitter. The people might tear that apart along with everybody they found inside the building.

How dumb, Steve thought.

The brains behind the entire complex scheme must have known the people wouldn't accept a dead woman as the resurrection of their heroes. They . . .

Steve stopped. He was partway along the side wall when he looked into one of the offices that blocked off the windows from the common workers who sat every day at their assigned desks, cut off from the sun and bathed in the operating-room light of overhead fluorescent bulbs.

Eric Von Kamp was alone in the office.

In front of him on the desk was a typed sheet of paper. He was reading from a script in a faltering but intelligible Spanish, memorizing the words but acting as if they left a bad taste in his mouth. The language seemed strange coming from a man with a German accent.

At the sight of Steve, he put down his paper.

"Leave me alone," he shouted. "I do what I must. I have to go through with it."

"Go through with what, Mr. Von Kamp?" Steve asked.

"You failed, not me," he shouted. "I warned you. I gave you a chance to save all of them somehow. Now it is left to me to do."

"What are you talking about?"

"The shuttle, you fool. My daughter's life."

Steve entered the office to hear better. The entire third floor echoed with shouting and screaming, changing quickly into a chant that beat at the ears.

"Perón. Perón. Perón. Perón."

Von Kamp put his head down in his hands.

"There really is a bomb aboard the shuttle?" Steve asked, wanting confirmation.

With his hands still over his face, the older man nodded.

"And you put it there, helped put it there anyway?"

Von Kamp looked up sharply. "No! I called NASA minutes after I was told about it."

"Then who put it aboard?"

"They!" Von Kamp took in the entire Peronist movement with a sweep of his hand. Then he seemed to make the final surrender. His body shrank, folded in upon itself like a snake-skin deprived of its substance. "To blackmail me."

"Oh, bullshit. Nobody pulls off a caper like this to blackmail somebody with no more money than you have."

"It's not my money they want, you fool. It's all of Argentina. There . . ." He pointed to the door. "That's what they want."

Steve turned his neck to see a man about forty standing in the doorway. He had a somewhat Latin look. His hair was slicked back and his forehead was high. He might be wearing makeup, Steve thought.

And there was something familiar about him.

He looked like Von Kamp.

No, Steve corrected himself. The similarities were subtle, recognizable only when the father and son were seen close to each other.

The man looked like . . .

"Good God!" Steve said aloud. The man looked like the picture of Juan Perón, Argentina's long dead dictator. And Roy had seen him in California, dismissing him as a suspect. Roy had just checked too soon.

"Good evening, Eric," the man said with a smirk.

"Eric? Never!" Von Kamp rose, his fists doubling at his sides. "You will call me 'Father,' damn you. I may regret the day I ever conceived a beast like you, but here, you call me 'Father.'"

Steve's mind tried to fit the older man's reaction into what he already knew. Nothing clicked.

"Remember Carlotta, old man," the smirking face in the doorway said menacingly.

"Perón. Perón. We want to see the resurrected Perón," the people were demanding in the office and in the street. They could be put off no longer.

They wanted to see the resurrection.

The men touched Perón's look-alike gently on the arm.

"*Vamos, Don Domingo*," one of them said. "*Sus amigos te llamas*."

"Domingo Perón!" Steve said. His suspicions were finally taking on substance.

"President Domingo Perón!" Von Kamp's son grinned.

The father spat out his own interpretation. "Dictator Domingo Von Kamp."

Domingo's face twisted into a gargoyle of rage.

"You want her dead." He checked his watch. "Twenty more

minutes, old man, and your darling Charlotte will be ashes unless you do as you are told."

His friends eased him away.

Corpus Cristi dashed up to Steve. "We have him. A Perón. You see. You Americans are so cynical."

Steve ignored her and spoke to the German. "He's their resurrection? Your son?"

"Yes." Von Kamp crushed the sheet of script in his hand. "You and your friends had better try to escape," he said. "My son cannot allow you to live after what you have just heard. It might prove embarrassing."

Cristi said, "I do not understand."

Again Steve ignored her.

"You're going to pawn him off as Juan Perón's heir?"

"Not me. Them." He meant the Peronists. "Whoever runs them. The little people, they are so starved for hope, they will believe almost anything."

"But why your son?"

"Because it could almost be true. Perón knew my wife before she married me. They started rumors that she was his mistress or his wife. Maybe she was. I don't know. I don't care. I loved her. And that vermin is *our* son. He was born eleven months after my wife and I returned to Germany."

"I don't believe you," Cristi said.

Von Kamp looked up at her for the first time. "Believe what you want. All of you."

"My God," she said. "We have been fooled again."

"If Cristi here can't be tricked, then how can they hope to pull it off?"

Von Kamp rubbed a shoulder and arm as if they pained him cruelly. "I cannot prove when he was born. All the records in Germany were destroyed. My wife is dead. My parents. My sister. All the friends who would know the truth. All of them are gone. Some, I suspect, were killed recently just for this very night."

"How many Peronists know the truth?" Cristi asked.

"Their leader, whoever he is. My son. Myself. You two. No one else, as far as I know."

"None of us knows the leader," Cristi said. "We were told

it was the only way the workers could rise again, following a phantom until a Perón could take over. What fools we have been all along!"

"Birth certificates can be forged," Steve thought aloud. "A marriage license, too. Once the people accept him, they will not want to be proven wrong."

There was a louder cry from the street and inside the building. The roar was reaching insane proportions.

"There," Von Kamp said. "They have their Perón reincarnated."

Steve looked out. He could see over the heads of the people crowded into the conference room. In the lights illuminating the balcony, papers were floating to the ground from windows higher in the building.

"Copies of birth certificates," Von Kamp said. "Thousands of German birth certificates, showing Juan Perón as the father."

"Faked like the photo showing Perón with your wife."

"Yes."

"They won't get away with it for long."

"You're wrong. The people want to believe, and there is no proof to the contrary. They have their Perón."

"I don't believe people are so stupid."

"You forget they have me." He came over and stood at the office door.

The uproar had changed in the street again. It was definitely a different mood. Most of the mob had grown silent. Scoffers were in control.

"There," Cristi said. "There are already doubters."

"All part of the plan."

"Von Kamp. Von Kamp. El hijo de Señor Von Kamp."

"They're claiming he's a fake," Steve said. "Somebody knows he's really your son."

"I said it is part of the plot. Those shouting now were planted in the crowd, no doubt. You see, I am to be the final word, the proof. I'm supposed to walk out on that balcony and say Domingo was Perón's son, not mine. I'm the final indisputable proof."

"And they will believe you?"

"Yes, again because they want to. And besides, in this

machismo society, what man would deny his only son, admit his wife was not his alone unless it were the truth."

"And if you don't lie?"

"My daughter dies. Three good men die with her."

"That's how the space shuttle became involved?" Steve said.

"Yes. It shows how diabolical my son is and how much support his backers can buy."

Steve said, "They made it worse than a kidnapping."

"My brilliant son would destroy the only other thing with meaning in my life. The space program. A disaster now will be enough to set back the program for years, decades perhaps. I was even told that the destruction of the shuttle would be blamed on Cuba. What hell will that bring down upon the world?"

Steve leaned against the wall.

"Go tell the fools the lie they want to hear," he said.

"I would . . . to save my daughter. I would kill myself to save her, but they would only push the button if I committed suicide.

"So I must unleash a sadist on Argentina. All South America. My son is mad. Insane. He has kept his true self from the public for a lifetime. But he is Hitler reincarnate. Not Perón. He already has plans for exterminating the Jews, of capturing all of Spanish-speaking America. He'll kill anyone who stands in his way. He plans to work with Cuba. He will build atomic weapons."

"God, no," Steve groaned.

"That's why my son went to such lengths to make my dilemma impossible. He needs me. For five minutes—two minutes—on that balcony. And later. If I deny what I said, he'd kill his own sister."

"They might still destroy the shuttle," Steve said.

"Domingo would, if he could. But she knows nothing, and I can refuse to speak until the last second. I convinced them I would know the shuttle is destroyed if they betray me."

If the spacecraft could last until nine o'clock, it would be safely into its descent, Steve thought.

"But can I . . ." Words clogged Von Kamp's throat. "I helped one monster—Adolf Hitler. I can't give birth to another."

"You'd let your daughter die?"

"Yes . . . no. . . . Oh, God, I don't know. It's an impossible choice. But if one man had stood up against Hitler, regardless of his personal cost, think what could have been prevented."

"Two men," Steve said.

"Two?"

"You and me."

"No, save yourself."

"But we can't let them destroy the shuttle. We can't surrender an entire country, too. Aw, shit." Steve smashed his fist into his open palm.

Roy Borden appeared in the door. His face was red and flushed. Perspiration beaded on his brow, and his eyes flashed with panic.

"Steve!" he shouted over the general turmoil. "Time's running out."

"The big part hasn't started yet."

"What do you mean?"

"Señor Von Kamp!" one voice shouted, then another. They were coming for him.

"Steve, think! Seven minutes and somebody's going to push the button."

"That's only part of the trouble."

"We have to try something," Roy insisted.

Steve unconsciously felt the gun in his waistband. "I guess we play kamikaze and go for the broadcast studio. Maybe the real leader is back there somewhere. If we can't wreck the transmitter, maybe we can kill him in time."

"He would not be here," Von Kamp said. "He will take no chances with being discovered before he's sure his people are in power. The pig is no doubt somewhere else, somewhere safe. Safe with his transmitter."

Men reached the door; they shouted at Von Kamp, then pulled him from the desk.

Eyes fiery with excitement, Steve grabbed his arm and shouted at him over the noise. "What did you just say? About their leader?"

Von Kamp had to fight back to keep from being carried away. "I said he wouldn't be here. He'd be safe somewhere else."

Steve's face shone with excitement.

"Tell the people," Steve yelled. He grabbed Von Kamp's arm. "Give me all the time you can. Speak softly in generalities until the last possible moment. The people will be quiet. If you hear three shots, an explosion, any signal I can give from farther up the street, tell them the truth."

Von Kamp's eyes fixed on Steve. "And if I hear nothing."

"Then God help Argentina. Give them their Perón."

Von Kamp was gone, and Steve stood in place, stunned by his own commitment.

Chapter 22

"THERE goes fuel cell two," James Carlyle said into the mike. "We've run her out of juice, Mission Control. No longer have triple redundancy. Hell, we no longer have any redundancy."

"That's okay, shuttle. You don't need it." An attempt at reassurance came back.

"That's easy for you to say."

James Carlyle sounded sour.

"Believe me, Jim," Fred Yarkin said from Houston. "Going into the descent with one cell ups your chances two hundred percent."

"Coming around," Carlyle continued, trying to keep his mind on the computers that were turning the great ship around so her engines pointed to the rear. "Starting engines. There they go. We got a burn. We're losing speed."

"We can see, Jim. We can see. Hang in there. The boys tell me you'll be safe soon. With that bomb in the position it is, even an explosion won't be critical with two cells down if the last one has bled off enough."

Carlyle's response was bitter. "If the bastards don't push the button in the next seven minutes. If they aren't using some super explosive. If we get the engine fuel burned off before they blow, if we get enough retro fire to keep us from coming in like a comet."

"Jim, don't think of it. In seven minutes—"

"In six minutes, fifty-two seconds."

"Jim, don't do that to yourself. Jim. Jim?"

The sound from the headset covering Fred Yarkin's ears cut out. Shuttle Charlotte was no longer sending.

"Fred," a man shouted from across the sterile clean room. "We've lost contact."

"That's all right. They're in retro fire. The signal's not getting through the heat," a woman technician said, trying to soothe the terror threatening the room.

Self-control had been a way of life there for years. But not now. Men were swearing. One wiped away a tear that blurred his vision. A woman sobbed openly. Another man smashed his fist into the paneling of his display.

Six minutes, forty-two seconds, Fred Yarkin thought. They were dead already or they still had six minutes, forty seconds of exposure.

And who was helping? Not him. There was nothing he could do.

In the Buenos Aires broadcast building, Steve Crown ran for the stairs. He knocked over chairs and kicked wastepaper baskets in his rush.

His sudden flight brought resistance. Not having any idea why the foreigner had decided to flee, several young Peronists stepped forward to block his path. Steve decked one of them by picking up a heavy tape dispenser and cracking the closest head. Stunned, the boy staggered away.

Two more Peronists pushed Steve back over a desk. One saw his gun and made a grab for it. Steve's hand came up from the desk top with a paper spike braced against his palm. He drove the six-inch-long heavy needle down through the left shoulder of one attacker. Roy knocked the other man aside with a karate kick just above the knee. The man sank like a listing ship, screaming and holding his kneecap.

Cristi shouted in Spanish.

Most of the others listened to her, and she made it to the exit with the two Americans.

On the stairs, a guard one flight down heard the running feet and the slamming door. He raised his pistol. Steve leaped.

Tipping his head to one side, Steve hit the new interference with his shoulder. The man flew against the staircase wall, his head cracking against the plaster.

He wasn't unconscious, but the fight was gone out of him. He resisted no further when Roy picked up the gun and all three continued down, unimpeded.

Roy and Corpus Cristi trailed Steve, shouting questions.

"Where the devil are you going?" Roy yelled.

"To the opera," Steve replied.

They were down the two flights and into the street. Steve plowed directly into the backs of the Peronist guards who formed a semicircle around the entrance. He knocked one forward into the crowd, where he was swallowed up by the press of people. Roy hit another squarely in the back with his shoulder. The man dropped his weapon and reached for his spine. Roy shoved him aside.

A third guard turned; Roy held the pistol by the barrel and smashed the man's jaw. The cracking of bone put the guard out of commission.

Roy called to Cristi, "What did Steve say?"

"He says we go to the Teatro Colon."

"Why?"

"Quien sabe."

She stomped hard on the instep of a man attempting to prevent them from escaping. Another she disabled by reaching down between his legs and grabbing and crushing his genitals while pulling him forward sharply with the same tender parts.

Her victim dropped his gun and went where she pulled, his mouth open in a silent and startled attempt to yelp.

The crowd was quieting. Eyes focused on the balcony where Eric Von Kamp was about to appear.

Meanwhile the three were fighting, battling their way through the mass, Roy using his gun to fire into the air. That caused a temporary commotion and gained them a few yards.

"Stay together," Steve yelled.

None of them spoke again. They struggled forward like fish swimming against a powerful current.

Worse. They were swimming through a river of molasses. Like a nightmare, they could see the opera house ahead, but they couldn't seem to move. People were so intent on the balcony of the broadcast building and so packed together they could hardly spread apart for the threesome.

Except for the ruckus kicked up by the trio, an ominous quiet was settling over the street. All attention was focusing on the balcony.

Five minutes left. Steve read his watch. Four minutes, fifty-eight seconds.

"Goddamn, get out of the way. Move. Bastards. I'll shoot."

Steve waved his gun, aimed at the concrete, and fired. The ricocheting bullet hit someone, and the cry of pain gained him a few more yards.

Still, it seemed impossible. They were never going to make it to the theater in time, even if his theory was right.

Then an explosion boomed beyond the edge of the crowd. A hand grenade. Someone had tossed a grenade toward the crowd.

A soldier? Tanya? He laughed. Chances were it was Tanya. Give her a job and she did it.

"Aw, fuck!" Steve stopped and looked back toward the balcony.

Would Von Kamp take the explosive as a signal to tell the people the truth about their false idol?

No, Steve decided. Von Kamp would know it was too soon for Steve to have accomplished anything. And he wasn't yet on the balcony. He was stalling as long as he dared.

Another grenade. Panic set in on that edge of the mob.

People began to back off. They wanted to run too.

"The army's coming!" people shouted in Spanish.

Steve repeated the cry. Then Roy and Cristi too. In seconds there was room for them to run. They strong-armed anyone who tried to stop them, but they were moving fast now and toward the block that was completely covered by the giant theater.

Then, when Steve thought they were going to make it easily, a soldier at the edge of the crowd appeared. He lowered his old rifle with bayonet in place.

"Stop!" Steve yelled.

Too late. The soldier thrust, and Cristi ran onto the short bayonet.

She gasped. "Ah-h-h!"

The blade was long enough to stick through the back of her blouse. Blood poured out front and back. All four stopped. Cristi's hands folded over the front of the gun barrel. The soldier, his eyes wide with fear, tried to swing the gun toward Roy Borden, who was bringing up the barrel of his pistol.

The body on his bayonet was the soldier's undoing. He couldn't pull free, and he couldn't maneuver the muzzle fast enough.

He pulled the trigger, blasting another hole through the small girl's midsection. Still the bayonet held.

Roy, normally never a brutal man, shoved his gun barrel directly into the soldier's mouth, knocking out teeth that dropped from his lips like the fakes used by comics as part of their routine. Roy pulled the trigger.

The army man looked surprised. His cheeks puffed out, as if he had been caught with a mouthful of forbidden fruit.

Then his head came apart. Most of the gore burst through the top, but the temples burst too. The impact lifted him off his feet, leaving Roy's gun and hand wet with blood and pieces of human flesh.

Steve saw Cristi on her knees, the bayonet still inside her. He bent to help her, but she pushed his hand away.

"*Vaya*," she ordered. "Go."

"I'm sorry." Steve knelt beside her.

"Go, damn you."

"Cristi . . ."

"*Vaya. No tiempo.* No time."

Roy's hand pulled at his friend. "Come on, Steve."

There's nothing to be done for the girl. That's what he meant. There'd be no getting an ambulance. Probably no chance to bandage her. Besides, the bayonet and bullet must have pierced vital organs. Her mind was just outliving her body.

Steve rose sadly. The girl meant nothing to him personally. She was just a girl, an adventuress. But for a while they had fought together. It was a shame her adventures had to stop so early.

"Steve, Steve!" Tanya Horton called from behind them.

He and Roy turned to see Tanya running across the vacant street, her purse weighing down her right shoulder.

"I saw the commotion in the crowd. I thought that might be you," she said.

Steve ignored her and bolted up the steps of the opera house. Roy was right behind him.

"What's so heavy?" Roy nodded at her purse.

"More grenades," she said. "I can't believe it. I killed a soldier. Lord, I hope this is worth what we're doing."

Steve tried a door and found it locked. He tried a second and then another. They stretched the length of the building.

"Here's one," Tanya cried, holding a door open.

Steve and Roy darted through it.

"Where are we going?"

They entered the waiting room for the banks of ticket booths.

"Just toss the grenades if we get him," Steve yelled at her.

"Get who?"

She looked at Roy.

He shrugged as they burst into the vast lobby. "I don't know. Just throw them in the street if we get anybody."

"This is crazy."

"Of course. What did you expect? Steve is running this show himself."

The interior was lit but empty. Stained-glass windows rose beside the stairwells. On the domed ceiling an enormous modern painting surrounded the massive chandelier.

The three agents darted across the foyer, each taking a

separate entrance so they came into the horseshoe-shaped auditorium itself down three different aisles. The lights were on.

Seats for four thousand people filled the ground floor and the seven balconies that rose in tiers like a huge wedding cake. Some house lights were on, dimly exposing the interior.

Before Steve could react, he heard two shouts. One cry came from a guard stationed an aisle over from Roy. It was followed by a shot that sent the guard stumbling back among the seats.

He seemed to bounce between the seats in front of him and those to the rear. He fell once, disappeared, rose again, and took a few more steps before he went down.

His wrist hooked in the space between two seats, and his fingers formed a fist as if it were making one last grasp at life.

Another cry came from a second man with a gun. He was high up on one of the balconies. He had a rifle and took a shot. It missed Steve by inches, but Tanya had crouched in her aisle, taken a small pistol from her pocketbook, and was bracing it for better aim.

She fired. Her bullet missed by a foot. The range was hopelessly long for the small gun, and the light was inadequate, but the marksman tossed away his rifle and stood with his hands held in the air.

Wisely, Tanya didn't fire again. She had the man terrified. If she shot again and missed, he might realize how safe he was and go for his own gun again.

In the same wild moments, Steve focused on the scene.

Down front sat perhaps two dozen men and women, all richly dressed as if they were prepared for the opera. They swung around in their seats at the sounds from behind them. Then they froze.

On the stage was a projection-size TV screen. Eric Von Kamp filled the picture. He held the sheet of paper in front of him, his face a portrait of indecision.

At the edge of the brilliantly lit stage that held the screen was a desk with a microphone and several pieces of electronic equipment.

The button, Steve guessed.

Somewhere on the instrument panel was the button, the

switch, or the microphone that could send a deadly signal to the space shuttle.

A foot to the left of the desk was Miguel Romonas Marcelo de Juárez.

He was the last to know his sanctuary had been invaded. Blinded by the footlights and deafened by his own self-importance, he finished his sentence.

". . . now we shall have Perón. *Our Perón*. In one minute, we—" he said in Spanish.

He had heard the shots.

"It's Steve Crown, Don Miguel," Steve announced.

He was moving slowly down the aisle, holding his gun with both hands directly in front of him. He had to get closer, much closer. There was no hope of hitting his target with one shot from such a distance.

"It's over, Don Miguel," he said as he moved.

"What is over? What do you mean?"

Marcelo's voice faded. On the TV set, Eric Von Kamp was being introduced.

The crowd was silent.

"Sixty seconds," Roy called from the other aisle.

"Go throw the grenades."

Tanya turned to leave.

"No!" Roy shouted.

Steve understood the warning. He was too far from Marcelo for a shot.

But time was running out. Von Kamp couldn't stall much longer. There were only seconds left. Not minutes.

"Go!" Steve ordered Tanya again.

She glanced nervously at Roy, then ran up the aisle and out through the foyer.

"What is this?" Marcelo asked. "What are you doing with guns?" He was nervously glancing at the TV screen, then at Steve.

"I got to thinking, Don Miguel. Who had money and power enough and connections in the American aerospace industry to pull off the rigging of a bomb aboard the shuttle? You, Marcelo. Your connection with Crown General was part of your goddamned scheme."

"*No comprendo*," the man on the vast stage said.

"And who was old enough to know about Perón and Von Kamp and Maria Gallardo?" Steve kept talking and walking. He had the gun in both hands and was ready to shoot regardless of the range if his target made a move toward the instrumentation. "Who was able to keep track of me from the minute I landed? Who tried to get me killed repeatedly? You, Marcelo. You even used your own daughter in your plot."

"Steve!" Anjelica Marcelo spoke from the small audience.

Oh, Christ, Steve thought. Why did she have to be here? What if he had to kill her father?

"Steve, my father, these people, they want the best for Argentina," Anjelica pleaded. "They—"

"They want to rule," Steve replied. "Even if they have to fool the people. That was another thing. I figured out the one group that might want to regain power but knew they never could in a free election. The oligarchy. The top two hundred families. But you could rule behind a Perón, couldn't you, all of you?"

From outside there was the muffled sound of an explosion, then a second grenade going off.

"Brilliant plan," Steve said. "You almost got what you wanted."

Eric Von Kamp's voice came from the TV speaker.

The audience was obviously held in rapt silence. The tension came through. All those thousands of people, and not one of them making a sound.

"He is not Perón. He is my son," Von Kamp announced softly in Spanish. Then louder. "He is my son."

He had just wrecked the entire elaborate plan.

Arms reached for the old German, yanking him from in front of the camera, but there was an uproar in the streets, the anger of thousands being expressed as one.

The small audience in the theater gasped too. Marcelo started toward the desk and the transmitter. "You meddler!" he shouted. "You have ruined a brilliant plan."

"Don't move," Steve shouted. "Or you're a dead man."

Marcelo stopped. His eyes tried to see beyond the lights.

The controls to the transmitter were so close. The radio here probably relayed to the broadcast building, where equipment would flash the simple signal to the edge of space.

Seconds remained. Marcelo was weighing what to do next.

Try to get out of Argentina before the mob or the military junta discovered his involvement.

Or push the button first. Four heroic people would die for nothing. But he would have his revenge, if nothing else.

"You win," Marcelo said softly. "With seconds to spare."

Then Marcelo moved suddenly, jumping for the instruments. Steve fired and missed.

Anjelica screamed.

Miguel Marcelo ducked instinctively as the bullet zapped past him. A moment later he was up again, standing straight and still. Would he make another attempt? Steve wasn't sure.

Then his wristwatch sounded its alarm.

Marcelo made a move, attracted by the alarm or taking advantage of the distraction.

Steve never knew.

The alarm warned him. It was still possible to kill the astronauts. He shot, then shot again and again.

He kept shooting until his gun clicked on empty, and then he reached for the spare clip he had in his pocket. He hardly knew what was going on around him.

Then he saw Marcelo's face bloom crimson, the bullet or bullets ripping away the nose and taking an inch or two of the cheeks along. The eyes seemed to pop out, then were mercifully hidden in blood.

Marcelo was miraculously still alive, a hand on the desk, holding himself up, the other hand fumbling for the switch that would destroy the shuttle.

Roy was shooting too.

Anjelica came running up the aisle,

Steve knocked her aside and fired, using most of the second clip. The last slugs spun Marcelo away from the transmitter. Blinded, he staggered with his hands out, caught the edge of a curtain, and let himself sink slowly to the floor of the stage.

Suddenly the opera house was silent.

Steve lowered his arm. He stood with his gun hanging at his side. Anjelica stared at him, looked to the stage, and sank into an aisle seat. She sobbed quietly as her mother rose and walked up to her husband's body and began praying over it.

The people in the front left their seats quietly. They hurried up the aisle and out of the opera house.

Steve could understand why when he looked at the large TV screen. The camera was still focused on the balcony and showed people fighting, clawing at the phony Perón, Domingo Von Kamp.

The father of the man who would have been dictator was no longer in view.

Steve could only hope the old man would be spared.

The sounds from the TV speaker were terrifying. It seemed that the mob was literally tearing apart those who had attempted to pawn off a phony on the nation.

Steve raised his wrist and looked at his watch.

Forty seconds past nine. The shuttle was safe.

And Roy was on the stage dismantling the transmitter just to be sure.

There was no one left in the vast auditorium except the Marcelos and the two Americans.

"All right," Steve called to Roy. "Let's go. Let's get the hell out of here while we can."

He touched Anjelica's shoulder. "I'm sorry," he said. "If you knew how your father intended to get Von Kamp to support his plot, you would understand. I had no choice."

She looked up at him coldly. "I knew about the shuttle all along," she said.

He shook his head. "Then forget the part about my being sorry. Play with other people's lives and eventually you lose your own."

"That goes for you, too, Steve Crown."

The comment made him pause. True. Sooner or later, he was going to get killed.

But he couldn't stop. Someone would need him again. There was always someone who needed help.

Roy joined him, and they walked up the aisle and out into the street. Tanya had a car and was motioning to them from the street. Somehow she always managed to have what they needed most.

"Hurry," she said. She was right. The police, the mob, or the army would be coming soon. None of them would ask questions before reacting, once they found the bodies in the opera house. There would probably be no gratitude from the Argentines of any political stripe. The Americans had given them a chance at a free election, but nobody would believe that. You could blame anything on *norteamericanos*.

Steve walked to the car.

It was over.

The shuttle would be coming down now. A glider silently rushing home to earth.

There was nothing more for him to do.

Except get on an airplane. Get a drink.

Maybe make a pass at Tanya Horton.

Yeah, he liked that. It seemed like a good idea.

About the Author

DAN STREIB is a world traveler, a gun buff, and an aerospace communications specialist. He is a full-time writer with over 49 paperback books to his credit.